Praise for the *Heaven* trilogy

heaven

A Coretta Scott King Award Winner

★ "Clear evidence that love, more than blood, makes family."
—*Kirkus Reviews*, starred review

"Believable, unconventional characters and friendships combine with small town fondness in this tale about the search for identity—an endeavor leading to more questions than answers." —*VOYA*

"Johnson writes of African American families and communities, mentioning here and there the shade of brown skin, perhaps the dreadlocks, that identify her characters' racial identity. This is a part of them, but certainly not the whole of these incredibly whole folks that Johnson has created." —*Kliatt*

the first part last

A Michael L. Printz Award Winner
A Coretta Scott King Award Winner
An ALA Best Book for Young Adults

★ "Readers will only clamor for more about this memorable father-daughter duo—and an author who so skillfully relates the hope in the midst of pain." —*Publishers Weekly*, starred review

★ "Brief, poetic, and absolutely riveting, this gem of a novel tells the story of a young father struggling to raise an infant." —*SLJ*, starred review

★ "Johnson makes poetry with the simplest words in short, spare sentences that teens will read again and again." —*Booklist*, starred review

sweet, hereafter

★"Johnson's evocative yet starkly simple language powerfully shows the devastating effects of the war on one small community. . . . The characters and circumstances are never anything less than rich and real."
—*Kirkus Reviews*, starred review

"This thoughtful tale, with its quietly poetic sensibility and timely themes, will resonate with those who are grieving the loss of loved ones." —*Bulletin of the Center for Children's Books*

"Johnson . . . uses spare, gorgeous, realistically raw language to bring to life a complex teen of great depth and heart." —*VOYA*

ALL THIS

AND

HEAVEN

TOO

ALL THIS
AND
HEAVEN
TOO

Includes *heaven*, *the first part last*,
and *sweet, hereafter*

Angela Johnson

SIMON & SCHUSTER BFYR

New York   London   Toronto   Sydney   New Delhi

An imprint of Simon & Schuster Children's Publishing Division
1230 Avenue of the Americas, New York, New York 10020

SIMON & SCHUSTER BFYR is a trademark of Simon & Schuster, Inc.
For information about special discounts for bulk purchases, please contact Simon & Schuster Special Sales at 1-866-506-1949 or business@simonandschuster.com.
The Simon & Schuster Speakers Bureau can bring authors to your live event. For more information or to book an event, contact the Simon & Schuster Speakers Bureau at 1-866-248-3049 or visit our website at www.simonspeakers.com.
Book design by Tom Daly
The text for this book is set in Garamond 3, Aldine 401, and Aldine.
Manufactured in the United States of America
This SIMON & SCHUSTER BFYR bind-up paperback edition January 2014
4 6 8 10 9 7 5 3
Library of Congress Control Number 2013939819
ISBN 978-1-4424-8719-2

heaven

to Kevin

April 28

Sweet Marley,

I'm on my way to Kansas. I guess me and Boy have finished our stay in Oklahoma. I decided on Kansas because of a dream I had. I dream so much now.

How about you? Do you dream of faraway places and the people who live there? Do you dream of the things you have done or might do?

Do you dream of me and Boy?

We dream of you. . . .

We dream and think of you and your family living in the house across from the river. (And yes, before you say anything I happen to know Boy dreams about you. I read him your letters, and he knows who you are. He's an evolved dog.)

About my dream . . .

I'm riding along in my truck and I pass a little boy on the side of the road. He's pointing ahead. I stop the truck and ask him if he needs

a ride anywhere, but he just smiles and shakes
his head. He keeps pointing, though.

As I ride further down the road, I see you
and your mom holding up signs that say
KANSAS. Both of you are wearing long dresses
covered in sunflowers—pointing. . . . There's a
gentle wind blowing, and your sign blows out
of your hand. (Then Boy woke me—he wanted
a snack.)

It was like you were really there, Marley.

Did you dream on the fifteenth of this
month?

Maybe you'd dream-skipped to Kansas. . . .

The land of sunflowers and Oz is calling to
me. I can't wait to get there. The sunflowers
will be in full bloom by the time Boy and I
show up.

Boy has decided to change his personality.
I'm still checking on the new one. When I
truly know what all the changes are—I'll let
you know. (But he has become a vegetarian!)

Looks like the oil wells go on forever in
Oklahoma . . .

Much love,
Jack and Boy

Angela Johnson

part one

heaven

In Heaven there are 1,637 steps from my house to the Western Union. You have to walk by a playground and four stores—two clothing, one food, and one hardware coffee shop. After you pass those stores, you cross one street and hop over a deadly looking grate. (I once heard about a man who got struck by lightning while standing on one.) Ten steps past the grate is Ma's Superette.

(If you can't find it at Ma's . . . she even sells live bait on the side.)

Ma's Superette is open 23 1/2 hours a day. Ma closes it from 4:10 A.M. to 4:40 A.M. every morning. She uses the half hour to pray. At least that's what she says she uses it for. When I said differently one day Pops said I was skeptical and not spiritual at all.

That made me mad 'cause hadn't I put all my allowance in the Salvation Army kettle last winter? Sometimes Pops just doesn't get it. He even said a while ago that because I was just fourteen I didn't understand about life, but I wasn't about to hear that. Sometimes he gets so mad at me, he just shakes his head and mumbles that I'm just like Uncle Jack. Then he tosses the thought away I guess and smiles at me, every time.

Anyway, Ma's was the place you could get nachos and nail polish, Levi's when you needed them, and flip-flops for the summer. I'd already gone through two pair and it's only the middle of June.

Heaven might sound pretty boring to most people, but before I really understood about all my years at the Western Union, it was fine for a girl like me.

I don't get sent to Ma's for bread and milk like most kids, but to wire money. I've been doing it ever since I've been allowed to leave the yard by myself. It's something I thought most kids did. It's something I found out a little further down the road that made me different from every other kid in Heaven.

postcards from uncle

We live in Heaven 'cause about twelve years ago Momma found a postcard on a park bench postmarked HEAVEN, OH. On the front of the postcard were clouds and a group of people floating around and waving. It said, HI FROM HEAVEN.

Momma said she'd been looking for Heaven her whole life–so we moved: Momma, Pops, Butchy, and me.

Pops was looking for another job, too. He said it was getting pretty dry out west. Too many people had decided California was the place they had to be. So it was time to go.

But this is how Momma tells it.

"Wasn't much to it. Small town, lots of trees and kids running everywhere. There was the cutest little school sitting over by the river–and when the Impala died right in front of this little house with a picket fence and Marley started screaming to go to the bathroom, we were in Heaven to stay."

Pops says, "What? I don't know. That was ten

or twenty years ago, and how am I supposed to remember any of it? I was almost blind from driving and about out of my mind with sleep. . . . What were we talking about?"

My brother Butchy grunts: "Do I look like the answer man?"

But Momma's telling is only the beginning of how we ended up in Heaven. A postcard, a dead Impala, and a house with a picket fence is only part of what got us here.

Why Momma was looking for Heaven is another thing. People look for what they think they need, I guess. You find what you think you need and what might make you happy in different places with different people and sometimes it's just waiting in a tiny town in Ohio with a cute little schoolhouse by the river. Heaven was waiting for us.

If the whole truth be told, that's adding Pops's truth and the little bit that Butchy knows—I figure we ended up in Heaven because of the postcard, Western Union, and Uncle Jack.

There aren't Western Union offices everywhere, you know. Sometimes you have to go miles to find one. When the car broke down and Pops needed a phone, he had gone to Ma's Superette, called a tow truck, bought bologna sandwiches, and had seen the Western Union sign by the register. Then he'd looked around town and thought maybe it would be a nice place to raise a family and pets.

The story is, between the ages of two and ten I had twelve dogs, fifteen cats, nine rabbits, ten birds (eight being nursed because of cat attacks), one lizard, and 105 goldfish.

Pops say I'm just like his twin brother, Uncle Jack, about animals. It's just not home without something furry or scaly or feathered around. I'm just like Uncle Jack, who's been everywhere in the world and who I only know through letters and the Western Union. . . .

May 8
Marley Marley,
Hey, Angel! How's it going in Heaven?
If that last hat that I sent you doesn't fit, make your melon-headed old man stretch it out for you.
Aren't you a little young for real big hair? Although I was about your age when I wore my first Afro. Didn't they come back in style for a minute?
Kansas is beautiful. Western Kansas is even better than the rest. Last night I slept on top of

Angela Johnson

my truck. Boy did, too. His tail wagged all
night long. We could see the world that night.

Ever seen a prairie dog, Angel? They're
quick, and Boy got pretty content just sitting
around listening to them at night on top of the
truck.

Did you know Kansas has incredible
sunflowers? I'm thinking about hanging
around until they all start to bloom.

Can you see them, Angel?

Hundreds of thousands of them waving in
the fields.

Can you see them, Angel?

They're tall and languid. Tall and
graceful. They're yellow because they swallow
up the sun and brown in the middle—almost
burnt from eating up all the rays.

Sunflowers all around . . .

Plant these seeds in a place Boy might like
to take a nap under.

Your uncle Jack (in Kansas)
and Boy

Uncle Jack hasn't seen me since I was born. He was
in Ohio a few years ago. He said nobody was home
for two days. Butchy figures that was the weekend

Momma and Pops dragged us to Cleveland to the museums, fireworks, and a rib burn-off.

That was also the weekend Butchy fell off a pier into Lake Erie after visiting the Rock and Roll Hall of Fame. He was playing air guitar and had us all falling on the ground laughing. We got hysterical when he disappeared over the pier until we looked down into the water and saw that Butchy was still playing. He swam to the beach and kept on playing long after Mom had thrown a blanket around him.

Now that's entertainment.

We'd stayed at a hotel downtown (I can't remember the name of it) and had walked around the city most of the first day, counting people wearing Cleveland Indian T-shirts.

We'd even run into a couple of people from Heaven. They were eating ribs at the burn-off in The Flats. (The Flats used to be old warehouses right off the river, but now artists lived in the buildings and festivals were held in the streets.)

Mom and Pops had stood around and talked while Butchy and I stuffed ourselves with elephant ears and french fries. It was a good weekend.

I know it doesn't sound too cool, but I like to hang out with my family. They're a good time.

Angela Johnson

I wonder what he looks like, my uncle Jack? Pops has one picture of them both. They were in diapers—sitting in a vegetable garden with an old dog at their feet. The writing on the back of the picture says: 1950 THE BOYS AND BOY.

Pops says that he and Uncle Jack have had about eight dogs named Boy. That makes Boy part of the circle, just like the rest of us are, but some of us are just finding out what our part is.

shadow ghosts and cadillacs

Shoogy Maple sees shadow ghosts and had been kicked out of every school she'd gone to. Then she moved to Heaven. Her family moved in across the playground last year.

Shoogy wears frosted lipstick and cutoff T-shirts (even in the winter) and knee-high rain boots wherever she goes; and she mostly goes with me.

We met at Ma's. She was buying a Slurpee and a burrito and putting money in a can to help rebuild churches that had been burned in the south. I was wiring money to Uncle Jack somewhere in Utah and wondering if Ma would let me use her bathroom.

Shoogy started scooping the beans out of her burrito and feeding them to Ma's cat, who was standing in the bin of flip-flops.

Ma grinned at her and went over to do the paperwork on my wiring.

I scratched the cat's head.

Shoogy said, "I like this cat. She's not afraid to

mooch. Most cats will just look at you like you're trying to feed them poison."

Not Ma's cat. She'd break into your house and drag the refrigerator across the lawn if she could.

This cat was notorious in the neighborhood for being the biggest beggar in the business district. Everyone fed her, and she was so fat, I didn't know how she'd managed to hop into the flip-flop bin.

When I said this to Shoogy, she howled so hard that she dropped her Slurpee.

Ma shook her head, put a roll of paper towels on the counter, and I helped the laughing girl clean cherry Slurpee off the floor. And when the cat started fighting us for the last of the Slurpee we both started laughing and screaming.

In the end we all got kicked out—cat included. On the bench outside of Ma's we introduced ourselves and laughed till our stomachs hurt.

I'd liked Shoogy on the spot.

Anyway—that's how we met. The reason we became and stayed friends was that she wasn't like anybody in her family and like everybody in mine.

Shoogy thinks the stupidest things are funny. She buys the worst tabloid papers (aren't all of them the worst?) looking for alien abduction stories, then has hours of conversation with my mom and dad about them.

My parents love it.

Shoogy says she can't share her alien theories with her parents. They get wrinkles in their foreheads and smile like they're in pain.

I guess the Maples are pretty dry.

Pops says that you shouldn't judge people too harsh, but I could sit all day in the middle of the street judging Shoogy's family and not get tired.

The Maples are "too" beautiful for Heaven.

They all have perfect heads and perfect teeth. There are two boys. Perfect. Two girls (off to camp tomorrow)—besides Shoogy. Perfect. And two perfect parents that smiled at everybody like mannequins and kept the most perfect yard in town.

Heaven is a pink flamingo, woolly sheep in the front yard kind of place. . . .

But the Maples got landscapers and awed everybody on Center Street. I'm pretty sure I was the only person in the whole town who judged them, though. You can pretty much do what you want around here and nobody says anything.

And then there was the way Shoogy acted when her family was around. . . .

Like a few months ago in March. Shoogy and me were hanging out of the tree in her front yard when her family pulled up in a brand-new car.

Shoogy said under her breath, "They went and did it again."

Then she somersaulted out of the tree and stood in front of the car with her hands in her pockets and her rain boots dug in.

I'm still hanging from the tree and thinking the big new car is pretty cool—considering it probably depletes half the region's fossil fuel, like our Impala does—until Shoogy kicks at the front of the grill and stomps down the street.

Six perfect Maple heads turn and watch her go.

I'm surprised at Shoogy. Surprised and worried a little about why a dumb car could make her so mad.

It was a couple of days after kicking the Cadillac that Shoogy started seeing the shadow ghost behind Pops. She said if you just glanced at the ghost, you'd think you were having double vision. But . . . if you stared at it for a while, it became a shadow with a warm glow. Following Pops.

Over and over Shoogy described the shadow, but I never saw it. That seemed to really get on

Shoogy's nerves. Shoogy said she had never seen a ghost before. She blamed it on living in a town called Heaven.

I blamed it on her being overheated wearing those rain boots all the time.

But even Pops's shadow ghost didn't keep Shoogy from still hating the green Cadillac. I sat in the car one morning while Mr. Maple beamed at the side of it. It looked like an airplane inside, and the seats felt better than the first-class airline seats I sneaked into once on a trip to New Mexico.

Mr. Maple said, "She's a beaut."

I nodded my head and looked across the yard at Shoogy as I reclined the automatic seats. You'd have thought I was drowning puppies by the way she looked at me.

Shoot! Not too many people in Heaven had automatically reclining seats in their cars. I'm pretty sure those seats made Shoogy hate the car even more. In her mind it didn't belong here. I don't think she thought her beautiful family did, either.

"What were you doing when you were eight, Marley?"

Angela Johnson

Shoogy and me were sitting on the sliding board and not letting any little kids go down it.

"I don't know; getting on Butchy's nerves and going to second grade, I guess."

Shoogy lifted her leg from the slide like she'd been burned. She took off her boots and tossed them under the slide, then she gave the little kids playing a nasty look—daring them to touch.

Shoogy says, "When I was eight, I was in beauty contests."

"Beauty contests?"

"Yeah. Why not?"

Shoogy got up and walked up and down the slide like she had a book on her head. Her frosted lipstick sparkled in the sunlight.

She has a drawer full of frosted lipstick.

"I used to walk like this, then like this."

Shoogy puts her hands on her hips and struts up and down the sliding board. She puts a fake smile on her face and blows kisses to all the kids on the playground. The way she walks the slide, her cutoffs and T-shirt could be a ball dress. Then it came to me—under that old wool hat and behind those dark plastic sunglasses, Shoogy Maple was beautiful.

I don't trust her family now. Something isn't right with all that perfection.

It makes me wonder why Shoogy stopped being beautiful and started hating Cadillacs.

Uncle Jack came up with a list of code words for giving the Western Union—he says he prefers them and that they work better for him. Says he doesn't want to carry a picture ID around in his pocket. He says he's lost so many wallets, he can't count them. (He leaves them on diner counters and in rest rooms.) So he gave each day of the week a special word. If money is wired on a certain day of the week, he uses that code word to pick it up. No need for a driver's license picture. The words:

> Monday—Sacrifice
> Tuesday—Truth
> Wednesday—Power
> Thursday—Beauty
> Friday—Life
> Saturday—Memory
> Sunday—Obedience

I had them memorized by the time I was six. The words I didn't understand Momma explained to me.

I wonder what Ma at the Superette thought of

me then, my note from Pops allowing me to wire the money, and the way I recited the word. I stood on tiptoe looking at the jawbreakers next to the register, hoping Ma wouldn't forget to give me one. She never did.

Uncle Jack's words.

That's all I know of him. His letters and the words he's lent to us to be a part of him.

Sometimes after I'd left the Superette, I'd lean next to the outside wall and imagine my uncle Jack. If I closed my eyes at the right moment I could see him.

Sometimes he's a grown man on a lonely country road writing on a piece of paper. Other times he's the shadowy baby in the picture surrounded by vegetables, his brother, and his old dog.

Mostly, though, Uncle Jack is just shadowy.

to the amish

Sometimes when Bobby Morris's car is working and his baby Feather is awake and not cranky, we take off to the Amish.

It's one of my favorite places.

Bobby once said that if it wasn't for Pennsylvania he'd only be forty minutes from Brooklyn. He'd be able to live in Heaven, and still visit what he used to know.

Bobby says he's always felt kind of Amish— kind of isolated from everyone, moving around at a different pace. The Amish have got each other, though. And Bobby's got Feather.

Feeling kind of Amish with Bobby and Feather is always a good time for me and Shoogy when Heaven isn't enough.

It's the greenest grass along Route 608, and the car rolls along with Feather in her car seat singing to the radio. We know when we get to Middlefield because Bobby always turns the radio off and rolls down his window. The smells are sweet cut grass, farmyards, and horses. . . .

Bobby lives over Canvas—they frame stuff, and I don't know how they make any money in Heaven, but they've been there for years. Anyway, Canvas beats the car repair shop Bobby used to live next door to. Here it's quiet and bikers don't come around there to drink beer and rev their engines at 1:30 in the morning.

Bobby put a flier up last winter at Ma's looking for a baby-sitter. What the flier said was:

LOOKING FOR A DEPENDABLE, BABY-FRIENDLY
PERSON. REFERENCES. TRANSPORTATION.
MUST KNOW "YOU ARE MY SUNSHINE"
AND LIKE *Sesame Street*.

The flier was purple with a pencil drawing of Feather in a diaper. Bobby says me and a woman named Trudy (who smoked like a chimney and asked him if Feather minded a little noise, 'cause she bowled four times a week at the Pro-Lane Alley in the mornings) were up for the job.

I started watching Feather the second week of vacation.

Feather was easy to fall in love with. The first time I saw her, Bobby was holding her and greeting me with a peace sign. They were surrounded by walls the same purple as the flier. Feather looked like her picture, tiny with wispy hair and caramel skin. A feather. Bobby and her mom must have named her after they met for the first time.

The purple walls made me feel at home, and Shoogy felt the same way after she'd come in off the steps to meet Bobby and Feather. Momma had Shoogy come along in case Bobby turned out to be a kidnapper.

That's Bobby, and even though he has purple walls he says that plain and simple are always the best. That's why he likes Route 608. The smells and the sights.

Plain and simple.

"Feather likes rhubarb pie more than almost anything," Bobby says.

She proves it by trying to shove a whole piece into her mouth. She's eating the pie and calling the cows that surround us "kitties" and "dogs."

"It looks it," Shoogy says, then wipes blueberries off her rain boots and lies back in the grass.

As far as you can see there's nothing but grass and barns. We sit in our favorite field next to an old barn that looks like it's been deserted for a hundred

Angela Johnson

years. It holds nothing to feed the cows and it doesn't look like it'll stand up to the next rain.

Furniture stores all over Ohio have been taking the old barns and making chests, tables, and bookshelves from them. Everybody's advertising "reclaimed barn wood."

There's enough falling-down barns in Ohio to put furniture in every house in this part of the state.

Bobby licks his fingers and Feather's, too—'cause he has no choice when she sticks them into his mouth as she crawls over him to go after some dandelions she's spotted.

Bobby moans, "She likes dandelions almost as much as rhubarb pie."

We watch her as she hides the butter-yellow weeds in her pull-up diapers.

Bobby finishes up his pie and says, "She looks like her mother."

"Did she eat flowers, too?" I ask.

Bobby adjusts his glasses on his nose and smiles. "No, but she was one." Then he looks at Feather as if she is the only baby in the whole world. Sometimes I catch Momma looking at me and Butchy that way. But Bobby never talks about Feather's mom.

The two people I like most—outside my family—

have secrets that I don't ask about. Momma says it's a flaw. She says I should be more interested; that people like to be asked about themselves. I should find out what made them who they are.

I look at Shoogy and Bobby and think it doesn't matter 'cause the past doesn't always make sense of the present.

Sometimes Shoogy drops hints about what she did before her family moved to Heaven. But Bobby never says anything. It looks to me like you're either born in Heaven or you come here from someplace else to start all over and forget what happened before.

Across the road four Amish women in dark blue dresses push mowers to cut their yards. They mow back and forth in their dresses, black stockings, and white caps. We all watch, and they don't seem to notice that we're even there. Even Feather stops picking dandelions. A cow moos off in the distance and Bobby reaches over and picks Feather up.

She squirms out of his arms, dashes as fast as her little legs can carry her, falls, then gets up and starts running and pointing again, this time to the women mowing the grass.

The sound of the push mowers echoes on the

Angela Johnson

hot June evening and the only other sound is the occasional cow and car passing on the road.

It's almost perfect.

Feather stops running and pointing and turns around to start pointing at her dad. Bobby is to her in ten strides.

He says, "It's almost like a movie. It's so perfect."

Feather eats a dandelion and says, "Perfect."

letter from uncle

May 24

Marley,

Yesterday I met a man whose father was a cowboy in the early 1900s. He died when the man was just four years old, in a riding accident. The man says what he remembers most about his father was the sound of his voice. Can you imagine that? Can you imagine remembering a voice from a hundred years ago. The man says he couldn't remember what his father looked like, but he could remember the voice that talked him into riding his first horse and taught him how to write his name.

I was sitting along a lake yesterday trying to recollect if I could remember the voices of people who were gone. I surprised myself. I actually heard some—well, a couple, really.

I remember the voice of the man who saved my life by dragging me out of a Vietnamese

river. I had never met him before. He died
going back into the river for somebody else. I
remember he kept saying that everything was
going to be just fine. He kept saying, "Just
fine, man, just fine."

Anyway, I've started hearing that voice
again, and that's almost been thirty years.

Can you even imagine thirty years,
Marley?

Can you imagine even twenty. I couldn't at
your age 'cause twenty was an age I never
thought I'd see. But that's all tied up in the
voices, too.

How is Heaven and your family in it?

I like the picture you sent me of your friends
in the field of cows. Those were cows, weren't
they? I think that your friends must be
interesting people. The kind that I would like
to know.

Do any one of them practice a form of
ancestor worship? I only ask because that baby
looks like she's been around the world before. A
very old soul.

I believe that Boy may be getting old. He's
not slowing down or anything like that. It's
just that he no longer looks at people or other

heaven   31

*animals like a young dog would. He seems to
judge a situation or person before getting
involved.*

*I mean—I taught this dog to be trusting of
people. It's always worked before. Now he looks
at me like I'm two years old, as if to say—let
me handle this.*

Such is life.

*I've been thinking lately that I should
maybe settle down and stay in one place for
more than a few months. (Don't tell your
dad.) I saw this family the other day that
looked so happy. They were sitting on the side
of the road eating ice cream. They'd pulled a
quilt out and just sort of took over the area by
the parked car as a picnic spot.*

*They laughed and waved to passing cars
and had themselves a good old time and I
thought—me and Boy do that every day.
What must it be like to go home to a house
that you've lived in and bought things for.
Things you love surrounded by the people you
love.*

*Anyway, all that just made me think of
you all—so I decided to write. And what
with Boy acting a little standoffish with
the world. . . .*

Angela Johnson

*Oh, yeah, to answer the questions from your
last letter.*

*The picture I sent you was of a dinosaur,
hot-dog stand. Good dogs, too. There's a whole
town of dinosaurs and things like that in
Arizona. You should see it. Little kids almost
can't stand it. They get so happy.*

*Yeah, I play the guitar well. I know it
looks good in pictures, but I can truly play it.
Doesn't your dad still play his? We learned
together. He was always better at it than me.*

*And yes, one day I will just show up in
Heaven and surprise all of you. I mean, what
fun would that be? You get so few happy
surprises in life. . . .*

*Let my coming there out of the blue be one
that you won't forget until I'm way gone out
the front door. Love to your dad, mom, brother,
and anyone who means anything to you.*

*Your uncle Jack
and Boy*

hitching

*Y*esterday Bobby picked this man up about four miles outside of town.

Momma said, "He must be crazy giving rides to strangers the way the world is today."

Then she mumbles something about what kids don't ever think will happen, but she grins and winks at me.

"Don't hitch, my girl. Okay?"

I grin back at her.

Hitching.

Most people in Heaven think that anyone who doesn't live here must have something wrong with them. It doesn't interest many of them what other people do outside of town, but when new people move in and get settled, they can basically do no wrong in the eyes of Heaven.

So as I'm pushing Feather down the sidewalk to the park, I'm thinking how the people I hang around with have been here less than a year, and they fit into Heaven just fine. And even while I don't know what I'd do without Shoogy and

Bobby, they sure aren't the people next door.

They're the kind of people who'd hitch to somewhere like the Natural History Museum and look at the stuffed animals, or to the Arcade to shop.

I take Feather out of her stroller and put her in the sandbox by the baby swings. The first thing she does is grab two handfuls of sand and pour them both over her head. I notice that the rest of the kids in the sandbox have the same beige covering their heads, so I figure as long as none got in her eyes she'll be okay.

I sit next to the sandbox and read a book about Montana.

"Nice baby."

I look up and smile at a woman sitting on the bench nearby.

I say, "Yeah, she is a nice baby."

"You baby-sitting?"

"Yeah."

"Do you watch other kids?"

"No, but do you need a sitter for your kids?"

She shrugs and waves to the sandbox when one of the kids stands up and shakes about fifty pounds of sand off himself. He runs over to us and leans against the woman.

She doesn't seem to mind that he's covering her

blue business suit with sand. She smiles off into nowhere and rubs the little boy's back until he toddles back to the others.

I look up every thirty seconds to check on Feather, and by the time I'm on my way to freezing to death with the woman in Montana it's time to go. The woman in the blue has already left with her little boy.

I figure no more reading at the park. Feather could have gone up the street and robbed a store or something in the few seconds my eyes are on my book. I don't think Bobby would be too happy. Parents in general are a nervous group.

I notice it in my own parents and strangers, too. It's like these kids are either bombs or precious gems to them. I don't think they know whether to cover them in something soft and keep them close, or just watch them carefully, making sure they don't do too much damage to the world around them.

Bobby has that cover-them-in-a-soft-blanket thing going on. . . .

Feather likes to fly, so I strap her into her stroller, surround her with pillows, and push her around the deserted parking lot by the feed mill like a crazy person. She loves it. In between screaming laughs she throws her head back and claps.

I stroll her back to my house, where we eat and wear most of her food. We look at all the commercials on TV. Feather loves any commercial with music in it.

By the time Bobby's car is pulling up in front of the house, Feather and me have had enough commercials and have pulled every dandelion there ever was in our yard. We have eight jelly jars full of them.

Feather starts pumping her arms up and down when she sees Bobby. He picks her up, smells and kisses the top of her head, and smiles.

"How's she been today?"

"Fine. I think she's been talking."

"What's she been saying?"

I hand Bobby a jar of dandelions and like his smell. He smells like paint and oranges.

"Oh, just baby things."

Bobby holds Feather and the dandelions close to him, and I start to see the resemblance. Feather still has a baby face that could change any time, but she already has Bobby's mouth and ears.

Feather turns to me and gives me her baby tooth smile, presses her face against Bobby's shirt, and falls to sleep in no time at all.

As I watch Feather with Bobby I have a picture in my mind of Pops and me washing his car. I must be about three years old. I'm making a big mess rather than helping, but Pops keeps smiling and letting me put soap back on rinsed parts of the car.

He just keeps rinsing and smiling. . . .

I ask Bobby if he's picked up any more hitchers.

He calls to me over his shoulder as he walks away. "Not today, but you never know what's gonna come down in Heaven."

Angela Johnson

part two

burning dark

$\mathcal{D}$own south they're burning churches. Pops says it reminds him of the early sixties. He says, "Mississippi," in a whisper and goes out back, sits on a lawn chair near the big old maple tree, and listens to the crickets.

That's what Pops does when he's about had it. Cricket listening.

Momma told me last week that they burnt down the church in Alabama that Pops and I went to when we were babies. She saw it burn on the news. She looked at me like she was going to tell me something, but stopped herself. She didn't mention that she'd ever been in the church. I thought that was weird.

Me and Butchy sit in front of the TV and watch another church fall down in flames. Flames that I can feel sitting a thousand miles away. Flames that I will feel long after the TV is turned off. Flames and the looks on the faces of people watching their churches burn down—burning hot into the night, burning dark when the morning comes up.

Butchy moves close to me. "They won't burn churches here, will they?"

I don't say anything. I look at him and see he's pretty scared about the fires. He moves off slowly to the back kitchen door like Daddy did. I'm left with the TV and Momma.

Momma crosses her legs and cracks her gum at the screen. She could stare anybody scared with the look she's giving.

"There's always going to be sick people, I guess."

Momma starts swinging her foot like she always does when she gets mad. That's the only way you know she's upset. Her foot swinging.

"But why churches now?" she asks like she's figuring out a math problem. I watch her like she might really know, like she has to know. I can't ask her, though. She might answer her questions, and I don't know if I want to know that much yet, but I got a feeling I don't have much to say concerning what I learn about the world.

Ethel Grabski always has our mail in the box by 1:30, every day. She's better than a clock as she hikes up the sidewalk in good walking shoes and the mailbag hung over her shoulder. She's been bringing us mail since I can remember. All five foot and beehive hairdo of hers. She smiles and wears what she calls blood red sea lipstick. She hands me the mail and stalks toward the next house.

Two letters for Pops and one for Momma, and a letter for somebody named Monna Floyd in care of Momma and Pops. I hand the mail to Momma while she talks on the phone about dry cleaning, then walk through the living room to my bedroom.

I don't ever remember Momma mentioning anybody named Monna Floyd. Stuff like this gives me what Pops calls the "nosies." I make sure I read the names and addresses of most of the personal letters that come to the house. (Just a thing I have, even though most of the time I feel like other people's lives aren't anybody's business.)

It's funny how you sometimes don't realize when you might be doing something for the last time. I didn't know it then, but that would be my last walk to my bedroom knowing anything about who I was.

I asked Bobby once what it was like to know Feather was really his, came from him, and was the closest person in the world to him.

He said it was important, of course, that she came from him, but people made too much of that kind of thing. They just did.

He was holding Feather's hand and kissing it.

He's one of those people who always says things like that. Somehow, though, I know he believes it. Even while kissing Feather's hand—I know he believes it.

It's a couple of hours later and I'm still thinking about Monna Floyd and churches burning down. I wonder if the Alabama-postmarked letter is from someone who's seen the burnings firsthand. It's like that six degrees of separation thing . . . everybody is closer than they think to everybody else.

I listen to the television as I hang over the side of my bed. The newscaster keeps going on about what a tragedy it all is—the church burnings. He also talks about how some of the burnings could be copycats.

I think it's a stupid thing to say. Burning something down for any reason is disgusting enough to stand on its own and not be thought of as something that's being repeated 'cause the idea was good.

A sweet wind blows in through my window,

and I can smell the honeysuckle. The sheer curtains float over my head, and I am just about to fall into a nap. Momma says I used to fight them when I was little. I'd stand straight up on my bed and refuse to sleep.

I guess naps are something some of us have to grow into. I remember thinking this as the smell of honeysuckle and the feel of smooth silky window curtains across my face, took me away.

If I dreamed in my nap I don't remember any of it. It was just a sweet summer sleep. I love the way I feel after a nap. I like that it's still day and I can hear Momma and Pops talking and the ice-cream truck coming down the street. Momma's and Pops's voices almost put me back to sleep until I hear Pops's voice raise.

I lay there until I hear the screen door close. I look out my window to see Momma sitting next to Pops. She's holding a piece of paper. Her head leans against his, and her eyes are closed. She soon lets the paper blow away. Pops gets up and follows it, reads it, and slowly looks up toward my window.

I wave and turn away and think how tall Pops is and how funny he looked stooping to pick up the paper.

storm

The sun is scorching when Momma comes into my room and lays down next to me on the bed. Her feet and legs hang over most of it.

"Do you think you might get out of this room before nightfall?"

"I had a good nap and woke up a long time ago. I just don't want to get up. The air is smelling so good here."

"The air always smells good here."

I roll on my side and look at Momma's face.

She has what Pops calls a classic face. Momma says that means she's not ugly or beautiful, just classic. I like that. I want to be classic like Momma.

Shoogy's beautiful. My brother Butchy's beautiful. I'm not jealous or anything. I'm okay about me. I've got a good face.

I touch the side of Momma's face and move a wisp of hair behind her ear. She just stares at me, then smiles.

She jumps up and heads for the door. "Get up, Marley—it's almost time to eat."

I watch Momma head for the door, then roll over on my back. She stops at the door and opens her mouth to say something, but nothing comes out. It scares me for a second, but she smiles and moves quietly out the door. The sheers blow across my face again.

It wasn't the storm, and it wasn't just that Butchy was supposed to come home and hadn't.

(My brother is two years younger and five inches taller than me. He hates organized sports and anything having to do with school. He says he'd be happy just to stay at his computer checking out the astrophysics Web site and hanging out at Junior's parking lot skateboarding with his friends.)

It wasn't even that Pops forgot about the fish cooking on the grill and let it burn, either.

It was everything.

It was one of those nights that started to go down before the sun did.

Me, Momma, and Pops end up eating hot dogs at the picnic table. Nobody's smiling by that time. Momma is trying to hide that she's staring at me, but Pops isn't hiding it at all.

I finally get sick of it and in the middle of a mouth full of relish and onions, I stick out my tongue at both of them. It works most times. Usually Momma tells me it's gross, and Pops shakes his head and tells me to keep my tongue in my head.

This time nobody says anything.

They just swat flies and keep on eating.

I say, "Guess I'll run uptown to see what Bobby is doing."

Pops says, "Uh-no."

"Why?"

"Because it's going to storm."

He looks up when he says it, and I notice the sky is a funny yellow color.

"I'll be back before it does. I swear."

When I get up to leave, Momma reaches across the table and grabs my arm.

"We said no."

I sit down and say, "Hell," under my breath.

"What?" Momma says.

"Nothing," I say, looking up at the yellow sky and sideways at Momma and Pops.

It isn't just the storm.

Oh yeah, it makes sense that we're in the basement now. The wind is knocking over lawn chairs and blowing the bushes around the side of the house.

The radio is saying a funnel cloud touched down over Middlefield, and I worry that the Amish don't have radios. I worry that they don't know what's coming at them. I worry that it's not fair and I can't do anything about it.

I sit next to Pops on the big cushy couch that's losing its stuffing. Anything losing its stuffing or missing a leg ends up in the basement rec room. I love it down here. Everything's comfortable and cozy.

Momma is sitting on the beanbag, as close to the radio as she can be. I guess it makes her feel better to be able to turn the volume up or down. I know she's thinking about Butchy, she's thinking about all the ways she can make his life miserable for worrying her during a tornado.

I don't want to think about it and fall off to sleep.

Pops wakes me. It's lightning out. I see it through the glass-block basement windows. I feel even sleepier, but I know something is wrong.

Momma gets off the beanbag and comes to sit on the other side of me, then I lean against her. All I can think about during the storm is the song "The Itsy-Bitsy Spider." It keeps going through my head.

Angela Johnson

Pops says, "Momma and me want to talk to you about something."

Down came the rain and washed the spider out.

Down came the rain and washed the spider out.

I remember later that night what Bobby told me. That the Amish trust nature to tell them when a tornado is coming. They trust the air around them and the way their animals behave. They watch the way the leaves blow and how the sky looks and the air feels. They trust nature to tell them what the man on the radio tells us.

I like that kind of faith.

I could have that kind of faith—in nature.

I now know how to watch for the danger signs, and I will from now on.

time

There's this movie where a man thinks he's the only human left on the earth. But he keeps living like he did when the world was full of people. He won't change. It's like, if his life changes at all, he'll have to look around and see the real reason why all the other people are dead.

I always watch that movie when it comes on. I always feel sorry for the man, too—every time.

Last night Momma and Pops kept saying that they should have told me what they had to tell me sooner. It's what people who haven't told the truth always say. From now on when I want to say something—I say it then. It's easier, and you won't have to think about it later.

It's strange how I couldn't take my mind off that letter and those church burnings. I'm thinking it started with Ethel Grabski delivering the mail yesterday, but I guess it started a long time ago.

July 20, 1996
Lucy & Kevin Carroll
34 Riverview Rd.
Heaven, OH 00127

Dear Mr. & Mrs. Carroll,
I received your address from a distant
relative of Mr. Carroll's here in Alabama. She
was kind enough to pass it on to my wife,
Pastor Anna Major.
I write this letter bearing sad news. It is
news that many congregations here in the south
have been enduring.
Our First Mission Church was burned last
week. It is a very dark time for us all.
Even with all this chaos I am in the process
of trying to re-create some of our files that were
badly damaged. Sadly, your niece Monna
Floyd's baptismal records were in the latter. I
would be grateful if you could send us a good
quality photocopy of the original certificate. As
Monna's mother, Christine, is dead, and her
father, Jack Raymond Carroll, is impossible to
find, I hope that you have these records.
We were so very fortunate that I could
re-create actual dates of baptisms, weddings,

and so forth from my wife's daily diaries that
span some twenty years, and that this diary
was in our home at the time of the fire.
 I hope that you can help us.
 May God smile on you.
 Deacon James David Major

And that was it.

Momma and Pops let me read it after telling it all. I almost felt the heat of the flames, flickering and scorching me way up here in Ohio.

When it was safe to come out of the basement, I walked up the stairs into a whole new house. Nothing looked or felt the same. I didn't have a place anymore.

I was like one of those people who gets hit on the head and doesn't remember anything, except past events kept coming to me, then disappearing again. They kept flying out of the pictures and furniture.

I caught glimpses of two summers ago when I was having a water fight with Mom and Butchy. I had a flash of Pops falling off the ladder while painting the house and covering the shrubs with paint.

Angela Johnson

I saw me as a little kid again, washing the car with Pops, and him smiling . . .

Nothing belonged to me anymore.

Momma and Pops had held my hand and told me the story in quiet voices and with sad, teary eyes. They'd said the right things and looked the right way while they were telling.

I stared at my hands and kept thinking, I thought I had my Momma's hands, and I probably did. It was just a different momma, one buried way down south in the cool red dirt of Alabama.

I want to see the movie about the man who refuses to change, soon. I guess I could rent it.

Maybe the man knew what made sense all the time.

I'd felt sorry for him because he didn't understand time. It moved on, but he didn't. He held on to a place in time that was gone. That's the thing about time—it's always long gone.

I didn't understand what the man in the movie did, that changes can drag you somewhere you didn't want to go. . . .

more shadow ghosts

It's been two weeks, and I still have not cried.

I decided while walking along the river, that the shadows Shoogy saw around my Pops—or uncle, or whatever—was a wraith. It followed him 'cause it knew what was coming. Maybe it was there to punish him for what he did and for what was about to come out.

It wasn't just a shadow ghost after all.

"Do you want spaghetti, Marley?"

Shoogy's house is all cream-colored walls and air that smells like apples. Fresh and clean. The kitchen sparkles until we show up and start making food. I have a feeling every room in the house sparkles until Shoogy makes an entrance.

Mrs. Maple wears a white tennis dress and smiles like a doll. She has perfect hair.

I nod my head about the spaghetti and watch the way Mrs. Maple smiles as Shoogy spills a jar of spaghetti sauce all over the counter.

Shoogy screams, "I got it," and smears the counter even more.

Mrs. Maple kisses Shoogy on the head and walks smiling out the kitchen with a tennis racket.

I say, "Your mom's nice."

Shoogy licks her sauce-covered elbow.

"Yeah, she's real nice. Always has been nice. Always will be nice."

"Nothing wrong with that," I say, meaning it.

Shoogy smirks at me with her frosted lips.

Past Ma's Superette and across the street from the bike shop there is a little alley that the town blocked off and put in some benches and flowers. They let the kids in the town grafitti the walls surrounding the garden. You'd think something like that would be ugly, but it's not. I think it's one of the most beautiful places in Heaven.

The walls get painted over once a month.

Everybody used to spray paint the overpass going out of town, and the city council thought this would be an alternative. It mostly is. Some stuff still gets tagged on the overpass—but I don't think the sprayers really put their hearts into it anymore.

Bobby is standing in the shadow of the left wall using a paintbrush. Feather sits at his feet making baby noises and pulling off her polka-dot socks.

Bobby doesn't turn around as I pick Feather up and take her to a bench. I smell her sweet baby hair.

"You ever think about using spray paint, Bobby?"

Bobby's brown legs are paint covered, and you can't tell where they end or his dark khaki shorts begin. He wears one of those safari hats 'cause he thinks it's funny. It is.

Bobby says, "Can't control the medium out of the can."

"Did you ever try?"

"Oh yeah." He laughs, turning around and looking at the opposite wall, then at me and Feather. "I was arrested in Brooklyn for it. I'm not fast enough for that kind of art."

"Was it real bad?"

"What, getting arrested or what I painted on the wall?"

Feather pulls my hair and tries to get down to get a bug. I let her.

"Getting arrested. I'd freak."

Bobby stops painting and turns around, smiles

Angela Johnson

and starts painting again. "I did freak. Feather was with a neighbor and she was definitely the type to punch 911 if I was late. Bad night."

"Some life," I say.

Bobby doesn't say anything else, and I watch him. He's painted over half the wall with black paint. He's not leaving it to the city.

I get on the ground and crawl around with Feather. She's managed to put a few things in her mouth while I'm talking to Bobby. She smiles and clamps her mouth shut when I try to open it.

Feather goes into a fast crawl to get away, then turns around and gives me the look Bobby always does when he is about to say something funny.

I remember looking at my hands and realizing that they weren't Momma's hands.

It would never be as simple for us as it is with Bobby and Feather.

I start to cry.

armed

*B*obby's arms are strong, and he holds me in them for a long time. Feather holds on to my feet and drools a little. Yesterday I told him everything. He fixed me soup.

Now he keeps saying, "Just think about today."

Bobby comes from what he calls a twelve-step background. He always takes everything one day at a time. He says tomorrow will come whether we're here or not.

So I try. . . .

I think only about today and how Butchy kept pounding on the bathroom door trying to get me to come out and the way he looked when he saw me walking up behind him after I'd climbed out the window. Then I try to only think about when Momma tried to talk to me and Pops tried to back her up and I only said, "Hell," and walked away.

I think of today when I walked by the river and thought about my father—Jack.

I just try to think of today, and Bobby's arms. . . .

Bobby says it's like this. . . .

You're this little kid and the first thing you remember is dropping a toy. Then somebody picks it up for you. Hey! It's that nice woman who comes when you scream or the funny man who throws you in the air and lets you eat the things the woman frowns at.

Then you know who they are.

Then you *think* they know who you are.

You do something stupid, they fix it. You're a kid, and they're the parents.

"Anyway," Bobby says, "it's just a matter of time before they get caught doing something stupid."

I say, "Bobby, this ain't funny."

He holds me tighter.

"It's not funny."

He holds me so tight, I can hardly breathe— then I start laughing. I laugh until I'm on my back in the alley.

Blue sky above and black wall tunneling up.

Feather crawls toward Bobby, gets within a foot of him, then curls up in the cool sand and goes to sleep.

"I hate them, Bobby."

Bobby takes off his paint-spattered shirt and covers Feather with it.

"Must be hard to hate people you've loved for most of your life."

I get up and walk over to the black shiny wall. He's started a painting. It's going to be a slow, steady painting. Bobby's going to take his time. He says that he once worked on a painting for a year and changed it about twenty times. He had to put it away.

I lean against the black wall.

"Happening wall, Bobby."

Bobby says quieter, "Must be hard to hate people you've loved . . ."

I turn to face the wall. "For most of my life."

Bobby lifts up Feather, who keeps sleeping.

I look at Bobby holding Feather and decide to leave.

"Later," Bobby says.

I run from the alley and head to Ma's.

I buy three purple pair of flip-flops, three different sizes, and head out into the light.

I drop a pair off at Shoogy's. I leave them with the twin boys, who are polite and say they will give them to her when she gets home from fishing.

Angela Johnson

I say, "Fishing?"

They say, "Yes, fishing," and smile at me.

I drop off Bobby's flip-flops at his door. I sit a while on the steps and watch people go in and out of Canvas, then leave when the sun starts going down.

Momma is digging in the front yard as I come up the sidewalk. She pulls her gloves off and waves me over. "Marley, baby, time to talk."

I stand in front of her, but don't say a thing. There's nothing more to say. Momma and Pops are my aunt and uncle and Jack. . . .

I don't have to say anything. I guess she sees I know it all in my eyes.

Momma stands up and puts her hands on her hips. I've seen her do that so many times, but this time is like the first time. I wonder how many other things will seem like the first time now. I keep moving down the walk into the house.

Momma doesn't stop me.

I go looking around the house for Butchy and finally find him in Momma and Pops's closet. I only see his feet as I walk into the room. He's buried his head way underneath a pile of sweaters that used to be folded and packed neatly. Sweaters are everywhere now.

I sit on the bed and wait for him to finish looking for what he wants in the closet.

The sweaters fall away around Butchy as he pulls out the metal box Momma and Pops keep all their important papers in. Then he looks up and sees me for the first time.

"What's up, brother?"

Butchy opens the box and starts going through the papers. He finds what he wants, looks at it for a minute—then puts it back in the box and shoves it in the closet. He hops up on the bed and sits beside me.

"What were you looking for?"

He puts his arm around me and looks at the closet. "Just making sure, I guess."

"Are you theirs?"

He slides off the bed and heads for the door. "Yeah, I guess so. But it's better to be armed with the truth, you know?"

I look at the mess in the closet and leave the room and just try to think about today.

Angela Johnson

dreams

I used to dream that a witch came through my window at night, walked over to my bed, grabbed me, and put me on the back of her broom. She'd fly down the stairs and head out the door with me. I'd always wake up screaming, only I'd never make a noise. Every time, though, Pops would be kneeling beside my bed, telling me the witch was gone.

He knew it, you know. I heard him tell Momma once. He knew the exact moment to wake up and go to me. I was so glad when I grew out of that dream, even though I missed Pops taking me downstairs and giving me a spoonful of peanut butter.

I miss that, but not the dreams.

I used to write my uncle Jack about my dreams, and he said he had a book that could explain all the dreams in the world. I thought that was it! A book to explain all the good and bad dreams. . . .

You can smell the water before you get to it, and all the houses look like little beach shacks. Lake Erie is close.

I turn and look in the backseat, and Shoogy is feeding Feather Cheerios and singing off-key to opera from the radio.

Bobby nods his head to an imaginary beat and lets about a million people cut in front of us when we get to Mentor-on-the-Lake. He calls it Zen driving, and we're all used to it.

We find the noisiest and most crowded place on the beach to put our blanket down. Little sticky kids run crazy on the sand. About seven different radio stations are being played from different parts of the beach. Sunblock, Kool-Aid, and all different-colored coolers remind me why I've always loved coming here.

> Me and Boy have been on the road so long, we feel like part of the pickup truck.
>
> Boy sits up on the front seat and barks at all the cows that we pass. He barks at cows, horses and, about ten miles back, at a truckload of chickens parked in a diner lot. Boy just wants some buddies. There's no meanness in him when he barks.
>
> Seems like we've been driving down this road for days. There are no hills and, for that matter, not too many things to sit on top of a hill. Suddenly, though, out of nowhere—to the left side of the road—there's a huge lake. Umbrellas

Angela Johnson

and little kids running around—probably
ignoring their parents—were everywhere. Boy
is going crazy.

We have to stop.

There's no sign about dogs not being allowed,
so we can sit beside the water and listen, and
remember.

Years ago we carried the baby in a Moses
basket onto the beach. She was so small, a woman
sitting under a gigantic hat thought that she was
a doll.

I remember that I covered her tiny feet in the
sand, and she gave her first real baby smile.

I remember that she made happy baby noises
when we both took her into the warm waters of
the Gulf . . . and the water was warm and the sky
a fierce blue.

I knew she'd always love the water.

And at the same time in Ohio . . .

Shoogy and Bobby play cards on the blanket
while I take Feather into the water.

One minute I'm standing Feather up in a little
tide pool, the next—I'm in a dream and the baby
is me. The sky is bluer, and the water warmer. . . .

part three

beauty

Shoogy says that once she had a screaming, crying fit in front of five hundred people on the pageant circuit.

Her momma always sat in a certain place—to the right and four rows back. She'd get one of the spectators to move or she'd make sure she got to the seat first.

Shoogy says she always counted on her momma being right there.

But when it came time for her to go out onstage and sing, for the talent part of the show, she couldn't find her momma. She stalled and looked everywhere. Finally she just gave up and lay down on the stage and started crying. She was six.

She was in a few more contests, but one day her momma found her in the kitchen slicing her thigh with a fork. The next time she had cut of all her hair with nail clippers. She said it took her a couple of hours. Her momma had thought she was taking a nap.

I don't think I'm going to have a screaming fit.

But lately, all of a sudden, my head will start hurting, and I can feel my whole body get so stiff, I feel like it's going to break apart.

I've been slamming a lot of doors lately, too. Momma hasn't said anything yet, but I know she wants to.

When I try to think about Jack my head hurts even more. After I told Shoogy about my parents and how I'm feeling, she said she had something to clear my head.

We're sitting on the walkway of the town water tower, swinging our legs over the side. Green treetops and electric lines lie under us. Shoogy lights up a cigarette she stole from her momma's desperate pack. It's the pack she keeps in the garage when she's about to go out of her mind. She quit smoking a year ago and still needs to know she can get to cigarettes real fast if she has to.

Makes me like Mrs. Maple a little bit more knowing she isn't so perfect.

I say, "Why don't we just go over to the high school and light up some of the jocks' sweaty socks and inhale them?"

Shoogy just laughs and inhales a few more times. "Do you remember anything about your uncle Jack—or your dad or whatever it is you are calling him."

I look over the treetops. "I don't remember anything. Except a couple of days ago at the lake, I think I dreamed something—that didn't really happen."

Since I didn't say anything else, neither did Shoogy. I liked that about her. Most people didn't 'cause she usually got quiet just before she did something crazy.

"What if I jump from this? Do you think I could make it to the treetop over there by the old town hall?"

I look where she's pointing and nod my head. "I hope you take your cigarette when you go."

Shoogy puts the smoke out and stands up on the walkway and howls.

"Hey! Shut up, they're going to find us up here."

But she keeps on howling, and I notice for the first time the deep gashes on her thighs, right over her rain boots. I watch her howl over the trees, over the wires, past the plane flying overhead, and away from Heaven.

Shoogy stops howling and looks at me. "Don't you need to howl? Howl at the people who screwed you over."

Angela Johnson

I shake my head and say, "Howl for me."

And she does. . . .

The red lights that surround the tower have lit up. Shoogy pulls out a sandwich and hands me half. We sit eating and watching Heaven light up through the trees.

I lean back against the H painted on the tower.

"I always wanted to go live with my uncle Jack when I was little."

Shoogy says, "Sounds like he has a cool life. Never staying in one place too long. Living out of a pickup, moving around with his dog. What did you say his name was?"

"Boy."

"Boy?"

"Yeah, him and Pops have had a lot of dogs named Boy. It's this thing they got for the name."

"Maybe you could still go live with him."

"Why would I want to go live with another liar, girl? It'd be just like where I am now. Living with people who lie."

Shoogy tosses the crust of her bread over the side. "Oh."

"Living with people who lie to you . . . and here I am thinking how I got everything okay at home.

I mean, I like my family. Look at you, you can't stand to breathe the same air as yours."

"Thanks for reminding me."

"Well, it's true."

Shoogy gets up and leans over the railing. "I think I see the floodlights from my backyard. My dad thought it would keep burglars out, but all it does is stay on all night. The raccoons play under it."

I say, "Thugs, here?" How would they find their way out to sell the yard sheep and pink flamingos?

Shoogy yawns. "Yeah."

I finish the last of my sandwich and watch as Shoogy walks around the whole tower. I can only hear her as she comes around the back, hitting the side. When I first saw the water tower, I'd told Pops that it looked like E.T.'s head. He laughed and told everybody what I had said.

I stand up and scream, "Hell," for about two straight minutes until my voice is about gone.

Shoogy just looks at me while I'm screaming, and even through the shadows I see a smile on her face.

"What is it about being high up that makes you want to scream?" I say.

"I guess up this high you really think somebody might hear you. I mean, they'll stop what they're doing, look up, and say, 'Hey, man! What's up with that screaming? It must be somebody in trouble. It must be somebody real.'"

I look at Shoogy in her dark glasses at night. "Do you feel real?"

"What's real?"

"I don't know anymore, I guess. It all got pulled away from me. What if *everything* Lucy and Kevin have been telling me all these years has been one fat lie? I can't trust anything they say now, can I?"

Shoogy shrugs and says, "I wouldn't trust 'em."

I say, "You're right. Who would trust them?

"Want to go to Montana? I read this book about this woman who goes there. I mean, she almost froze to death there. . . . "

There's a red glow coming from Shoogy's mouth, and smoke circling us. She says, "You want to go someplace where some woman almost froze to death?"

"Yeah, but it was real. She did it. She did it by herself."

"What's the big deal? Did she fly?"

"No, she rode a horse to Montana from Philadelphia back in the 1850s."

"I guess that's keepin' it real."

I say, "I hate this 'keepin' it real' stuff. What's

it all about, anyway? Real *is* what is. If you have to keep something the way it is, then it's not going with the natural flow. That's lying. I mean, if you can't change because you think this is the way it always was and anything else would be phony, that's stupid.

"I'm pissed at my par—Kevin and Lucy. That's real. The way I'm dealing with it is real. I mean I can't just say, I understand why you both lied to me for a crillion years. Yeah, everything's cool. I can't talk about it. It's too stupid and it hurts me too much. That's real."

Shoogy laughs. "I was just agreeing with you about the woman going to Montana. That's all."

I start laughing, too. "Sorry."

Shoogy says, "Yeah."

I watch the shadow of Shoogy. Then I say, "Do you think Jack would have kept me if I was beautiful?"

Shoogy throws her cigarette over the side of the tower, then puts her arm around me. "We're all beautiful—so who knows why he did what he did."

Angela Johnson

full

I wake up, surprised, to a cardboard box at my feet and wonder if it was Momma or Pops who put it here. It's one of those flowered storage boxes about the size of a shoe box that people put letters in.

I wake up easy, you know, and I don't know how . . . I must be real tired. So tired, I didn't hear them come in.

It's been that way lately—me sleeping till somebody has to bang on my bedroom door. Butchy usually comes in and hits me with a pillow. Momma knocks hard and says, "Up, girl," which makes me think of dog tricks. Pops just knocks and says softly, "Marley." Softly, "Marley."

I love the sound of my name now. Want to hold on to it and hear people say it over and over again. I never heard the sound of my own name coming out of me. I say my name a lot now. It holds me somewhere I used to be. It makes me feel whole and full.

I like that they named me after Bob Marley. Pops used to dance me around the house when I was little to his music. He used to dance me around . . . I'll never dance with him again.

Sleeping late is about not going down to breakfast and not saying the wrong thing. Not screaming, "LIARS." Not saying, "Was it worth it—making me so miserable now? Making me want to know why—and nobody can tell me."

Oh yeah, they can tell me that my mother really died. When I ask how—they just say she died and my dad, Jack, wasn't able to take care of me. Had too much sorrow in his soul and had to go away.

I know a lot of people with sorrow in their soul. Ma down at the Superette's got it. Why else would she keep that store open like she does? Never leaving it. Only stopping to get down on her knees and pray.

When I was little, I used to wonder if she put the Bible underneath her knees to cushion the pain from the old oak floors she was so proud of. I wondered if she'd lost a child or if her pain was that she never had one.

Sometimes when I was wiring money to Uncle Jack, I wondered if Ma made enough money at the Superette. The only person she had to help her was her nephew, Chuck. He was this biker who grew tomatoes and liked to hang out at the Old Towne Tavern. He's the only person I ever saw help Ma at all.

Chuck was better than a son to Ma and he wasn't her blood son. Ma seemed to smile only for him . . . and I could almost believe that you could love a niece or nephew as much as a son or daughter. Almost.

Ma had sorrow.

But I'll bet a whole bunch of money and anything that's important to me that she wasn't leaving kids for other people to raise.

I kick the box with my foot, and it falls over the side of the bed and hits the floor. I lie on my back and stare up at the stars on my ceiling. At night they glow in the dark.

Every year Pops replaces the ones that fall off or just don't glow like they used to. He put my stars up when we first moved to Heaven. I can remember telling everybody I met that I had stars in my bedroom. Then one day he put the moon there for me.

The stars and the moon.

My Pops would stand underneath them with me and look up at them like it was the first time he'd ever seen anything so pretty.

I'd do the same thing he did. Pointing at the

stars. Remembering if he'd put them in the same place as the last time.

He was never wrong. The stars always stayed in the same place. I have to remember that. I have to keep on thinking about that when I want to scream at Momma, Pops, and Jack.

Heaven is in a valley surrounded by farms and woods. There's a million places to go if you want to be alone and all of them are within walking distance.

I walk through the kitchen, and Butchy is washing dishes. Pops and Momma are gone to work. I turn back toward the fridge and grab some grapes out of a bowl.

Butchy tosses soap bubbles at the window. He says, "What's up?"

"Nothing."

"What's that?" he says, pointing at the card-board box.

"Something I haven't opened yet. Something Momma or Pops left in my room."

"What is it?"

"It says 'Baby Monna' on the box."

Butchy goes and sits at the kitchen table and looks scared. "You gonna open it now?"

Butchy hasn't been saying too much since I found him looking for his birth certificate in Momma and Pop's room. When he's around me he smiles. He always starts to say things to me but in the end always says, "Never mind."

He sits at the table banging a spoon. He's got his knee pads on already. He's been living on his board a whole lot more these days.

I saw him yesterday hiking up by Caveman Hill.

I went there once with him and his friends. Skinny boys with long shirts and baggy khakis. All of them looking for the perfect wave.

Caveman Hill will never be the ocean, but it slopes and dips through old twisted trees and burnt-out fields. Any minute you think you might see dinosaurs coming out of the dark night, getting in the way of the skinny boys on flying wheels.

I take a seat beside Butchy and shake my head. "I'm not opening anything now."

"What do you think is in there?"

I lay my head down on the table and close my eyes.

"You don't have to talk about it, Marley. I mean, after they told me, nobody's saying anything."

"It's all changed now. I still love you, but you aren't my brother. And at least if they'd lied to you, I'd still feel the same about you, because then you'd be going through these changes, too."

Butchy gets up, lets all the water out of the sink, and turns on the radio. He picks up the skateboard leaning against the pantry door and stands up on it.

He rolls out the back door, then stops. "We'll always be who we were to each other." Then he's gone to find the perfect wave.

Walking around town, I think about how the colors of everything have changed and it's like nobody has seen it happen.

They still put vegetables outside the Hahn Market.

Spin More Records still plays hip-hop on Saturday afternoons through the outside speakers, and classical music on Sunday mornings.

It's just that nobody has seen that the vegetables aren't as red or green as they used to be. The big album outside the record store is gray now instead of coal black. Nothing is as clear as it used to be.

I've been walking around town all day with this box in my hand. The cardboard is wet. I spilled a cherry Slurpee on it earlier. I almost left it on the bench in front of the hardware store where I watched Chuck, Ma's nephew, delivering tomatoes to different people on the block.

He has boxes and boxes of tomatoes in the back of Ma's Superette pickup truck. His arms flex his tattoos when he picks the boxes up. His smiling face says he planted and took care of these and now he'll feed everybody.

I don't notice him walking toward me. He stands there in a Harley T-shirt and work pants. Then he hands me a tomato almost as big as my head, and walks away.

I hold it, then put it on top of the box and look away. I think about Chuck and Ma, and when I look at it again, it's the reddest tomato I've ever seen in my life. Right there on Center Street. Right there beside me.

water

My Dear Sweet Marley,

*The other day Boy and I stopped at the
most incredible lake I've ever seen. I've seen
some strange things, so believe me when I say
this was one of the strangest.*

*In the middle of miles of wheat and other
things being farmed, I came upon a lake with
a beach surrounding it. The beach was
surrounded by a wheat field. If I hadn't been
in the pickup and a bit raised off the road, I
never would have seen it.*

*Boy must have sensed it, though. He loves
water and always knows when it's close.*

*The beach. What can I say about the
beach? There it was, where it was. . . .*

*I've never seen such happy people. They were
farm people who worked hard from sunup to
sundown, and you could tell that when it was
time for fun, they knew how to have it.*

*Maybe it just seemed to me that they didn't
take the water for granted. All those wheat*

fields and never-ending plains. You can see forever on the plains, Marley.

Some people say farming gets in your blood. They say that about fishing and hunting, too. I guess it all has something to do with controlling the natural world.

But you really can't control nature, Marley. You can reel her in and plow her and even kill a few of her creatures. In the end you can kill everything she offers or you can take what she gives you.

It's important to understand the natural world.

Anyway, Boy and I sat on the beach, walked the beach, waded in the water, and generally people-watched — kids running around not minding their parents and parents running after them or reading under beach umbrellas and relaxing behind dark glasses.

A funny thing happened while we were checking out the scene on Starlight Beach. Great name, huh? I asked a man selling ice cream why it was called Starlight Beach and he said, "Why not?" I liked that answer.

Oh yeah, the funny thing. Boy started following a group of kids around and wouldn't

heaven

*leave them. Even when they went on the far
side of the beach to play their boom boxes, he
followed. I let him go 'cause they seemed to
enjoy his company as much as he did theirs.*

*He especially liked a baby one of the kids
was carrying around, probably his little sister.
Boy always stayed at the baby's side. The
baby, of course, would pull his ears and sit on
him, but he didn't seem to mind. He stayed
right there while the kids danced the afternoon
away in the sand.*

*It reminded me of something from a long
time ago.*

*Boy cried when it was time to leave. He
whined and wouldn't come to me in the
beginning, but in the end he trotted past the
sand castles and picnic baskets, through the
fields of wheat, and got in the truck.*

*I felt bad for him as we pulled away from
Starlight. He looked out the back window for
miles. I guess he was hoping the kids would
follow.*

*Sometimes, Marley, I worry that I'm not
being fair to Boy. He's never lived anywhere
more than a few months. Maybe he needs a
yard and a house, where he always knows*

Angela Johnson

where his water dish will be. I know having one vet wouldn't mean anything to him, 'cause he hates them all, but maybe it would be easier. . . .

   Maybe someday I'd like to know where my water dish will be, too. . . .
   Peace and love from me and Boy,
   Love to your folks and brother
   P.S. Thank you for all the dog drawings. I think it's great of your friend Bobby to give you lessons. I've papered most of the inside of the truck with them. Boy is fascinated. He gets real low on his belly and paws at the one you did on yellow paper. Remember it? You stamped thunderbolts all around the edges of the paper.

the next door

*O*nce I heard Momma and Pops talking about a woman who used to work out of town and could only come back to Heaven on weekends. The woman had a baby that she used to leave with a sitter. The woman came home one weekend, and the sitter and her baby were gone.

She never saw her little boy again.

I was so little when I heard the story that I can't remember the name of the woman or if she still lived in Heaven. I just remember that I never wanted a baby-sitter.

Used to run screaming after Momma if she tried to leave me with one. Butchy used to follow me, saying, "It's okay, Marley, Momma's comin' back." He always said the same thing. Every time. He was younger than me, so how did he know?

How did he know?

Well, I guess he didn't know. Not only did my mother not come back, but another one took her place and didn't tell me that she wasn't the real one. I look at Momma and want her to be mine, really mine.

I feel bruised and motherless, even when I want to go to Momma lately and tell her it's okay. I just want what I used to have. But I can't. My legs won't carry me to her.

I miss her.

I put Uncle Jack's letter where I keep the others. I look in the bottom of the chest of drawers and run my hand through what seems like thousands of envelopes; all different colors and addresses. Some are written on motel stationary, and others were recycled from other people's mail.

I've been getting letters from Jack since I was a baby. Pops used to read them to me then. I learned to read when I was four—so Jack wrote them to me after that. I used to keep the letters in my toy box. Then I kept them in a Tinkertoy box, until it got too small.

I put the cardboard box in my letter drawer before I go to sleep. Unopened.

After carrying the box around for a few days, I got this idea that if I just threw it away, everything would go back to the way it was.

At Bobby's house, Feather uses it as a drum. She beats her baby hands on it and drools.

Bobby stands against his purple wall. "I'll stay with you while you open it."

heaven

I smooth Feather's soft hair and say, "That's okay."

"You not going to open it *ever*, then?"

"I don't know," I say.

Bobby goes into the kitchen and comes back with lemonade in tall, icy glasses. He says you can work through anything with something cold to drink in your hands.

He sits down cross-legged, and Feather crawls to him, begging lemonade. He lets her have a drop, and she puts baby floaties into his glass. He smiles.

"Why did your folks just drop this box off in your room? Didn't they want to be with you when you opened it? We're talking heavy stuff."

I take a gulp of lemonade and walk over to the window. A woman is dragging a huge picture down the street. I can't see what the painting is, but she's having a hard time with it. The door to Canvas opens, and the owner runs out and helps the woman get the painting inside.

"I don't know what to say to them, Bobby. I don't know whether to cuss 'em or hug 'em. I don't know whether to scream at them or stop talking to them. I think they know that, and that's why they're leaving me alone."

Angela Johnson

Bobby gives Feather another drop of lemonade before she crawls away from him and tries to take her diaper off. I look at her and wonder if my . . . Jack ever held me the way Bobby holds Feather.

Bobby gets up and goes to a canvas he's painting and turns it upside down.

"Don't say anything, then, 'cause you might say something that you'll regret saying. I know about that."

I walk across the white painted wood floor and stand next to Bobby. He doesn't talk about his life before coming to Heaven. I know he lived in Brooklyn and that he doesn't say that he misses it, but I can feel that he does. He's never talked about Feather's momma, but I feel like he misses her, too.

Must be sad to miss so much.

Must be sad to not know that you ever had anything to miss. Walking around in the world thinking you know it all. Thinking you know who you are. Walking around in the world like me.

Bobby's dreads brush my face.

He whispers, "When you're ready to open the next door to your life, I'll be there, if you want."

I lean against my friend, who's only a few years older than me and has a baby and some secrets of his own. I lean against him harder and watch the box a few feet away that might tell me secrets of its own.

Feather finds it again and this time she chews on a corner. When she's had enough of that she beats on it again and smiles a slobbery grin at me and Bobby.

I flash again on me and Pops washing his car. He is still grinning at me, but Momma has come into the picture this time. She's got a camera and she's saying, "Give Momma a smile, baby. Give Momma a smile."

Shoogy is in my room when I get home. She says the door was open and nobody answered, so she came on in.

"I like your stars," she says.

I put my box on the dresser and fall across the bed beside her. "You say that every time you come in my room."

She taps the side of her sunglasses and picks at some lint on my bedspread.

"I wanted stars like yours, but my mother said it didn't go with the decor."

"The what?"

"You know—the bears and other woodland creatures in *my* room that *she* decorated."

Shoogy pulls off her rain boots and throws them across the room. I see some of the same scars around her ankles that I saw on her thigh the other day.

I say, "You're not a bear kind of person. What's up with that, anyway?"

Shoogy goes over and turns on my radio to a hip-hop station and says she likes my Zora Neale Hurston poster.

She falls down on my beanbag chair and takes out a cigarette.

I say, "Not here, girl."

"Sorry."

She puts the pack into her rain boots and leans back to listen to the music.

Shoogy looks over at my poster.

"No, guess I ain't a bear kind of person, but I sure come from a bear kind of house. You're lucky. Your mom and dad pretty much leave you alone. They don't want you to be something you're not."

I look at Shoogy like she's nuts, but see that she's for real. She sees my parents like that. And I know I used to see them the same way. I remember that. It hasn't been that long.

"That box over there is what I am. They kept that from me long enough, don't you think?"

heaven   93

Shoogy stretches her legs out and looks up at the stars.

I look at the scars on her brown legs and then look up at my stars, too.

The stars were a good thing, and I could look around the room and see other good things. Something unseen made Shoogy do what she did to herself, but I'd never felt that kind of pain before with Momma and Pops. I'd only felt pain after I didn't know where I stood or who I was.

Shoogy gets up and tosses the box onto the bed beside me. I look up at her frosted lips and dark spy sunglasses. She kneels on the floor beside the bed as I open the box on the same spot where I found it.

Angela Johnson

momma

Shoogy told me when I first met her that she used to cut herself so it would block out pain. I didn't understand. She told me that she couldn't cut deep enough. I almost cried when she said that. And I wondered what could have hurt her heart so much.

We're both fourteen. We both like the same music and think the same things are funny. . . .

I open the box by ripping off tape and untying a thin pink ribbon that's been wrapped around it. Inside there's another box. The top of it says, AKNOCKMAN'S SHOE STORES, MONTGOMERY, ALABAMA. There's a piece of tissue paper covering everything except a tiny baby shoe.

Who I was sat in front of me.

Shoogy takes off her sunglasses and holds on to my arm.

She says at her old school there was this boy who made up this song called "Black Girl with Violet Eyes." Her violet eyes look at me, then the box.

My baby shoes are pink.

I lift out a tiny white sweater with pink roses stitched in and a tiny hat to match it all. Next comes a hospital bracelet with the name FLOYD, MONNA typed in on the space under NAME; mother's name CHRISTINE FLOYD. I hold on to it.

Then I close the box. There's more, but I can't look at it. I hold on to the sweater, hat, and shoes. I hold on to the bracelet and curl up on my bed.

Evening sounds wake me up, and Shoogy is asleep on the floor. We've both been covered with cool cotton blankets, and I can smell Momma's perfume in the room. The baby clothes and bracelet are still in my hands.

I walk Shoogy home, and a bunch of little kids in Halloween masks come running at us from the direction of the Community Center. They're having Halloween in July. All the kids probably have five pounds of sugar in each of them. Shoogy stares at the hundreds of little kids dressed as ghosts or butlers with axes through the heart as they run down the street.

She does a cartwheel right in front of Ma's Superette and screams, "It's just like Christmas!"

I listen to the kids laughing and watch the way

Shoogy looks, like she wants to go running after them.

In front of the Center, sombody's cut up a watermelon like a jack-o'-lantern, and there's lots of kids and parents sitting around eating sweet corn and hot dogs.

Shoogy decides to join in, and by the time I turn around and look back down the street, she's having Halloween in July with the rest of Heaven.

I walk back toward Riverview and twirl the baby bracelet in my pocket and feel better than I've felt in a couple of weeks.

Pops is sitting in the driveway as I come down the walk, still in the car wearing his work clothes.

Pops works in the lumberyard or, as he says, cuts wood for a living. "Cutting wood and wood-cutting," he always says. He says his job is what he does, not what he is. I asked him once what he was. He said the world's most famous thinker who hasn't been discovered yet. Then he laughed.

Pops leans out the car.

"Want to go for ice cream, kid?"

"Lactose intolerant," I say, and walk on by.

"They got Tofutti," Pops says, drumming on the steering wheel. I look at his round face and the wood chips in his hair, then go around the front of the car and hop in.

Pops pulls the Impala out of the drive and heads out of town.

"Aren't we going to the Dairy Queen?"

Pops stops at a crosswalk to let some masked kids cross the street.

He puts in a tape.

"You know what song this is?" he says.

I know it's jazz, but I don't know the name of the song. I just look out the window and watch all the fields and cows blow by.

"Miles Davis. Nobody like him, Marley. Nobody ever will be. . . . "

"Do you look like my father?" I say as the fields and barns outside of Heaven blur into one.

Pops turns off the music and looks at me.

He pulls at the name tag on his shirt. I have all of his old shirts. Every time he gets new ones, I grab the old ones. I like the way they feel big and baggy on me. They're all I'd wear if I could.

"The last time I saw Jack, we did look alike. He's taller and has bigger ears." Pops laughs at some joke only he and Jack would get.

"Why?"

"Why what, Marley?" Pops slows the car down

a little and reaches out to touch my arm. I move closer to the door, but not before I see the look in his eyes. It's like I just shot him.

"Why is this happening? Why didn't anybody tell me? You should have told me you all were raising me 'cause my mom was dead and my dad didn't want me. You should have told me when I was little."

Pops keeps driving and staring straight ahead. "Yeah, we should have told you when you were little, but not the things you think we should have."

I start kicking the passenger door. "Yeah, like you told me about magic and how one day I wouldn't mind having a brother."

Pops's voice gets real low. "Was I right about any of it?"

"I don't know anymore. Maybe the one big lie makes everything a lie."

Pops says, "Maybe. Maybe it does."

Pops used to do magic tricks for me and Butchy when we were little. I just naturally thought most kids grew up with their dad pulling rabbits out of hats and making vases and things disappear. When Butchy was real little Pops even made him disappear out of a hatbox.

I thought he could do anything.

One spring morning when I was five, me and my dog Holly were playing in the yard. A ball rolled out in the street, and Holly went after it. The lady in the station wagon never saw her.

I found out later Holly had probably died on the spot, but I didn't know that. I kept crying for Pops to make her come back. To make her stand up. Neighbors all around; and me screaming and hanging on to him.

Wanting magic and knowing he could get it for me.

Pops pulls over to the Tastee-Freeze on Route 306. A waitress comes over to the car to take our order. She smiles and pulls at her polyester uniform. I feel bad for her in the heat and sticky dress, so I order food and ice cream. Pops just orders ice cream and doesn't eat it when it comes.

We head home and don't say anything to each other.

When we drive by the YOU ARE ENTERING HEAVEN sign, Pops says, "It's always good to know where you are, I guess."

I move over closer to Pops. I say, "Sometimes I don't have a clue."

Angela Johnson

Pops says, "Sometimes it's easy to tell where you are. Just look around and notice the people who have always been there for you, and follow them."

I look out the window as we pass a poster on a telephone pole that says, SOUTHERN CHURCHES ARSON RELIEF.

Then I watch the last of the Halloween kids running home out the rear window of the Impala.

part four

love letters

$\mathcal{A}$ note I wrote to Jack.

> *Jack,*
> *Do you think about me like I'm your daughter?*
> *Do you think about me like that at all?*
> *Marley*

Then I tore it up.

Hadn't been down to wire Jack money in weeks. Mom and Pops stopped asking, and I stopped wanting to. Butchy does it now.

He wanted to know how we could give Jack so much money. So he asked. Pops seemed surprised, but told him.

And this is what Butchy told me. . . .

My mom, Christine, died in a car accident, and it looked like the car company was at fault. Jack got a lot of money. He got so much of it that it kind of freaked him out, so he put it all in the bank and let Pops deal with it.

Butchy says Pops told him he thought it was strange that neither he nor I had asked before. Butchy said he didn't ask 'cause he never thought about it. I just thought my parents loved Jack, and would give him anything. That's just me not knowing about money.

Butchy says Pops told him it all just like that, and I'm thinking to myself how easy it all would have been to tell me in the beginning. Just like that.

Alone in my room again, I open the Baby Monna Box.

Beside my baby clothes is a diamond ring in a velvet box and some letters Christine had written to Jack. I haven't read any of them yet. But written on the top of the envelope are the words LOVE LETTERS.

Bobby says people don't write love letters anymore. He says it's old-fashioned but kind of beautiful. Most people just go on the Net and e-mail who they love. I kind of think Bobby is old-fashioned in a way, that's why he knows. . . .

> *love letters. . . .*
> *love letters. . . .*

love letters. . . .
love letters. . . .

Petals fall out of the first letter. Just fall out and blow all around my room 'cause a breeze comes out of nowhere and carries the dark yellow flowers all over the place.

Christine liked yellow flowers. . . .

I am Christine's daughter, so that must be where I got my love of flowers.

The woman who digs in the yard now is my mother. Is not my mother. Is my mother. Is not my mother who I got my love of flowers from. She is not the woman who loved Jack, then died, and left him with a little baby. Me.

The hands I look at now are not the hands of the woman who digs in the yard. That can't be.

My mother is the woman who wrote love letters to my father who is not the man who works at the lumberyard and loves ice cream.

It's starting to be real 'cause there are love letters.

Angela Johnson

mountains

Today I put every penny I had into the church relief can at Ma's. I stuffed dollars bills into the can until Ma reached over and gently pulled my hands away.

Mrs. Maple broke her ankle playing tennis and had walked on it half a day before Shoogy's dad finally picked her up out of the front yard, put her in the car, and took her to the hospital.

The Caddy screeched down the road with the twins running behind it like their parents were never coming back. They walked back to the driveway holding hands.

Shoogy goes over and wraps her arms around them and it's the first time I ever saw her even seem like she cared for anybody who was related to her. The twins look at her and smile, then walk back to the house. Still hand in hand.

Shoogy sits down on the front yard beside me and pulls up big handfuls of grass and throws them up in the air. "She's always been like that," she says.

"Who and like what."

Shoogy lays back on the beautiful grass. She pulls out a piece of clover. Our yard is full of both of them.

"My mom is something. She never has pain or problems. Some people would call that perfect."

"Your mom's scary 'cause she doesn't complain?"

Shoogy rolls over on her stomach and pulls up more grass.

Shoogy says, "I'll never be like her."

She says it real sad, though, and that surprises me. I mean, Shoogy is beautiful like her Mom and everything. It's funny, 'cause I didn't think she cared to be like anybody in her family. The perfect Maples. Shoogy wanted to be a perfect Maple?

I start to see her differently.

I start to think it doesn't just roll off her back since she stopped cutting herself 'cause she couldn't be perfect.

The twins are running out the front door toward Shoogy.

I say, "Later."

Shoogy waves and puts one of the twins on her back. She gives him a horseback ride until they both fall on the ground laughing. . . .

Angela Johnson

I almost run into Pops as he's coming out of Ma's. He should be at work, but there he is munching on chips and sucking on a juice box like it's something he always does in the middle of the day. I get a hit of cool breeze from the air-conditioning coming out of Ma's. Pops smiles at me and offers me a chip.

We walk over to a bench outside of Ma's and sit down.

Pops says, "Had a few errands to run, so I took the afternoon off. So this is what it feels like to hang out in the middle of the day?"

"Yep, I guess this is it."

I look up the street. The music store is getting a piano delivered, and a woman pushing a stroller walks past singing a lullaby. Two doors down, the bookstore is having their windows cleaned.

"Guess I haven't missed much. What's up with you? Doing anything fun?"

"I thought I'd go over and pick up Feather. Bobby's working at home today. He's painting small signs, so Feather's probably covered in paint by now."

Pops hands me another chip. "You're a good friend, Marley."

I look at Pops as he finishes his drink box. He looks far away from Center Street and Heaven. He could be off in the mountains somewhere. He could be sitting on top of the highest mountain in the world.

"What were you doing at Ma's?"

"Errands."

"What kind of errands?"

Pops laughs. "Errands I can't do if I'm working."

"I could have done them for you."

"You going to keep bothering me? Is it that you have too much free time, or do you really care about the things I have to do?"

I laugh and say, "The first one."

I get up to go. Pop scrunches up his drink box and throws it in the trash can by the bench.

"Say hi to Bobby for me. Hi to Feather, too."

I look at Pops still sitting on the bench. He's gone back to the mountains.

Mr. and Mrs. Maple wave to me as they pass me in their car. A second later Mr. Maple has backed the car up and is smiling at me. I go over to the car. Mrs. Maple has a cast on her leg and is smiling like her husband.

Mr. Maple says, "We're having a cookout

Angela Johnson

tomorrow. Hope you can come."

"Yeah, I can come. Shoogy invited me this morning."

Mrs. Maple leans toward her husband. "Glad she did."

Mr. Maple waves another car around.

I just notice that the Maples are wearing the same tennis outfits. Mrs. Maple doesn't look like a person who just broke her ankle. Her hair is in a perfect bun.

She says, "I'm glad our daughter found you. It's hard for her to make friends."

I start to feel real uncomfortable in the middle of the street. I start to think the smiling Maples are going to have me for lunch. I guess my eyes are getting to look like a deer caught in the headlights, 'cause Mr. Maples says, "I guess we should be on our way. I haven't been into work today. Looks like a half day off is going to turn into a whole day."

I say, "Yeah, everybody's taking off today."

They smile and drive off.

The twins will be glad to see them; maybe Shoogy will, too.

I'm starting to think the family thing isn't as clear as I thought. The Maples. I can't get past the fact that they really love Shoogy. Perfect looks, house, and all don't keep them from seeing who she is.

Mrs. Maple's eyes got all watery when she was telling me she was happy Shoogy met me. I wish I could dislike the Maples more. I tried for Shoogy's sake, and the scars on her legs. . . .

Every day it all gets more fuzzy around the edges about the people who call themselves our families. . . .

I think of Pops, in the mountains.

Feather is only painted a little when I get to Bobby's. Bobby sees me and gets that thankful look on his face, then kisses Feather as I take her out the door.

After a moment he runs out after me with her stuffed diaper bag, gives it to me with a kiss on the head, and goes back to work.

Feather and I sit awhile on the bench by Ma's and watch the world go by. I think about folks as Feather falls asleep, dreaming baby dreams, and it's like we're in the mountains, too.

Angela Johnson

pop!

Instead of going to Shoogy's mom's picnic, I hang upside down in our maple tree out back eating Pop Rocks and thinking about how a lot of animals live their whole lives jumping around from tree to tree.

(Can't stand the thought of having too much fun. I feel too sad and shaky, so no picnic.)

I figure if I can stay up here a while, everybody will think I went to the picnic and leave me alone.

They're watching me, you know.

I started noticing it a few days ago. It's not only Mom and Pops watching me. Butchy is, too.

We'll be talking about something like skateboarding or comic books or how I'd been thinking about moving to Montana, and all of a sudden he's not talking anymore. He's watching me and waiting. For what, I don't know.

I think about it for a while and watch some squirrels on the ground looking up at me. I drop them a few Rocks and they sniff, then ignore them. I'm kind of glad they do, 'cause a squirrel eating Pop Rocks would not be pretty.

I guess if you think about it, a girl hanging upside down from a tree limb eating candy and getting paranoid about everything isn't that great, either.

Pop!

Angela Johnson

music

I feel a little better. It's three days after the Maples's picnic, and I think the tree helped—a little. I think sloshing my brains upside down for a couple hours knocked the cobwebs loose.

Feather and I had been listening to music all morning. By the time the sun got too hot, Feather started fussing, which isn't like her. She didn't eat her bananas and she wouldn't even clap when her favorite song came on the radio. So I figured I'd take her for a walk to Shoogy's house. I sang the Sunshine song all the way there. I messed the words up pretty bad, but Feather managed to babble in tune.

The twins are spinning in circles and running into each other as I stroll Feather up the sidewalk to the front door of their house.

I watch the twins fall down screaming, and I say, "Is your sister home?"

They look at me and laugh like they don't have good sense.

When I ask again, they laugh even harder.

So I take Feather out of her stroller and open the front door to the Maples's house. Shoogy's sitting in the middle of the living room floor with her legs crossed and flute music on. I only want to stay a few minutes, so I sit Feather on the floor and she aims her baby head for a huge glass vase standing in the corner. She's speeding up to a fast crawl— she still gets everywhere quicker that way—when Shoogy leans over and grabs her and lets her play with the newspaper she pulls from underneath the throw rug.

"Your brothers are–"

Shoogy rolls onto her stomach. "Strange?"

"Yeah, I guess. But what I really wanted to say is that they don't seem to need anybody else, being twins and all."

"They don't."

Shoogy stretches out, and I can't help but look at the cuts on her legs. It still bothers me. She says it shouldn't. She says I don't let enough go. I feel too much. I need to learn to do something about it.

"You don't still do it, do you?"

Shoogy asks, "Do what?"

When I point to her legs, she looks at them like they just attached themselves to her.

Then Shoogy just smiles at me and says that

Feather has probably eaten the whole sports page. By the time I get to her over by the couch, she's grinning newsprint.

"Was it good, Feather?"

She keeps on grinning as I pull about a ton of paper out of her mouth. She decided to store the paper in her cheeks instead of swallowing it.

Shoogy gets up, turns the flute music off, and puts on some rap music just as her mom walks through the front door.

At first I think it's a coincidence, but the look on Shoogy's face tells me different. Mrs. Maples doesn't look like she'd appreciate rap. She looks crisp, like she just walked out of a magazine, like she probably always smells good and never sweats. She's perfect.

And talking to me and I'm not even paying attention.

"I saved some of it for you."

I say, "Excuse me."

Mrs. Maple sits down on the white couch with Feather in her lap. Somehow she's got Feather, and the baby isn't trying to run. She just looks up at Mrs. Maple and grins, then leans her head against her and falls asleep.

Mrs. Maple yells over the music that Shoogy's

being kind enough to share with the neighbors. My mom would have just cut me a real nasty look and the music would have been off, but that doesn't happen here.

Mrs. Maple screams, "The pie, I saved you some peach pie. Sugar said it's your favorite. It is, isn't it?"

I scream back at her, "No."

She yells back at me, "Good. I'm sorry you missed the picnic. Is your grandmother okay now?"

I look across the room at Shoogy, and she's about dead, laughing. I don't think I've ever heard her laugh so hard before. And Feather keeps on sleeping, drooling on Mrs. Maple, who keeps shaking her head and hollering at me that she's already started taking calcium because she doesn't want to have the problems my grandmother has when she gets older.

It's all too much to take about my nonexistent grandmother and peach pie. I smile at Mrs. Maple and take Feather off her lap, then shoot Shoogy a real dirty look and get out of there.

It gets weirder and weirder every time I go to Shoogy's house. You couldn't tell it by just looking at them, but the Maples are nuts.

And sometimes Shoogy can be mean.

As far as that goes—so can I. I think I have more reason than Shoogy does to be mean. It's hard for me, though. I don't think I'll ever be too good at punishing people.

I push Feather's stroller back toward her house, and we start to sing "Sunshine" when somebody rides past us in a pickup with their radio on playing Feather's favorite song. She starts to clap her hands and smile. We walk past the truck, which is just parked by the hardware store, and Feather points at the dog who leans out the passenger window and looks at us both like he knows us.

letters

On Sundays we always get in the car and go some-place we've never gone before.

Pops whines about filling the tank up, and Mom says as long as we don't go back to the place that was supposed to make the best omelettes in the world. She was sick for four days after eating there. Butchy puts on his headphones and make-believes he's boarding down a smooth mountain. I used to think about my uncle and mountains and the places he went to and the people he met. I'd think about him and Boy.

If you think about how things might have been a long time ago if something had just changed a little—you might just bug out.

What if Christine hadn't died?

I've been carrying Christine's love letter around with me. The petals are falling apart in my pocket. I feel better with it.

We missed the Sunday drive last week because of Christine's letter. I couldn't find it just as I was about to go out the door. I tore the house up.

When I finally looked up, everybody was standing around me looking at their feet or the wall.

I threw the rug in the corner of the room, slid to the floor, and cried.

My whole body ached like I'd been punched.

I sobbed, "I don't have that much, you know. I just got parts of her back. Just the paper parts. The parts with words and ink. The parts that can be folded and stored. Folded and lost . . . it isn't just paper to me now. It's like my mother was holding me in her lap and letting me have the necklace around her neck. It was something I could take away that was part of her. And, and . . . if I'd known. If you had only told me when I was little, it would all be okay. I know it would all be okay."

Momma knelt down next to me and covered me with her body.

My heart hurt so bad. I fell asleep on the floor.

When I woke up, Pop and Butchy were moving the TV—looking behind it. Mom was going through the bookshelves just in case . . . just in case.

Heaven
I'm in Heaven
and my heart . . .

heaven

A letter from Jack.

Marley,

Yesterday, Boy and I slept by a beautiful river. We had spent most of the day in the St. Louis. I checked out a baseball game. I got tickets in a trade from a man in Indiana who liked this blanket I'd bought in South Dakota.

I thought about you as I sat by the river. I thought about what I would say to you—if I met you finally. I thought about how much you might look like Christine.

Do you hate me, Marley?

I was thinking yesterday by the river that if I was fourteen and lived in a small town and loved my family—I'd hate me.

I have been worrying about it a lot. Boy knows something's wrong. He sticks close and watches me when I cross the street. He stays close when I sleep, too. I must have bad dreams, 'cause sometimes I wake and find him looking me right in the eye. What do you think?

Incredible dog, or dog's hallucinating pal?

Do you think there would ever come a time when you think you might like to see me now?

Angela Johnson

I know things have changed so much for you,
me not being your uncle Jack anymore.
      I don't have to be your uncle, Marley; but I
certainly won't ever try to be your dad. You
have one who loves you, as I do. . . .
      Jack
      P.S. If you want to write me back, your
dad knows where I'll be staying. He'll
forward the letter to me.

I wrote back.

      Jack,
      I lost the petals and a love letter that used
to belong to Christine.
      Marley

Bobby asks me if I want to go to work with him.
I can take Feather along and let her play while he
works. He says he misses her in the daytime and
just needs to look over and see her face. He says
he'll pack a lunch for us tomorrow if it's okay with
me. I tell him it is.

      While I'm walking back home I can't help but
think how Jack had stayed away all these years.
Hadn't he ever wanted to take me to work with

him? See me in the daytime? Look at my face?

When I get home Momma is sitting on the front porch. When she looks up she's crying, and I run to her. Just as I'm about to get hysterical about Pops or Butchy she hands me Christine's letter. The envelope is a little dirty and looks like it had been chewed on, but the letter and petals are okay.

Momma wipes her eyes. "Found it under the tree out back."

I put the letter in my back pocket and sit next to Momma and notice I sit the same way she does, hunched over.

Then she says, "I loved your mom, Marley."

I nod my head and move closer to her. We wave away flies and watch the cars go by.

Angela Johnson

wings

*L*ast night I dreamed everybody I knew had wings.

Mom and Pops had huge blue wings; Butchy had green ones. Feather had little orange wings that moved like a hummingbird's. Bobby and Shoogy were fixing each other's wings with paste which they didn't think would work.

But there I was—wingless, sitting on top of a plane waiting for takeoff. I was mad at everybody else 'cause they could fly anytime they wanted, and they were all saying wings aren't always as great as you think. Pops complained that you couldn't get a good middle seat at the movies, and Mom said they were hell in the office.

I woke up smiling.

There are yellow ducks on the tiles in Bobby's bathroom. While he's giving Feather a bath she's pointing at the ducks and quacking.

I close the toilet lid, sit down, and wait for Feather's bath to be over. I start to read some of the storybooks Bobby keeps in a basket in the bathroom.

And I remember.

She's singing a song while I splash bubbles all over the tub. Every few verses I look at her and laugh out loud, splashing the bubbles more. Soon we are both covered in bubbles. She's singing louder when all of a sudden, a wet, bubbly dog is in the tub with me and I am laughing, calling out his name.

"Boy, Boy, Boy, Boy. . . ."

Bobby's painting a billboard outside town for a farmer who has lived in Heaven for ninety-six years. The old man says he loves the town so much, he wants to give it a present.

Bobby's been painting the billboard for a few weeks. It sits on a hill in what used to be the farmer's cow pasture. He only keeps a few cows now, around the yard to remind him of what it used to be like.

We load Feather up in her car seat and head off into the warm morning.

Bobby says, "On mornings like this, I don't even miss the city or my family."

Since Bobby hasn't ever really talked about his family that much, I'm a little surprised.

I say, "You've never really talked about too many people, Bobby."

Angela Johnson

He slows down near the river leading out of town to wait for a mama raccoon and her babies to cross the road. "Yeah, well, I got a few brothers."

"Parents?" I ask hopefully. I can't stand the thought of Feather not having grandparents any more than I can stand the thought of anyone not having parents. It makes my stomach hurt.

"Uh-huh. I got a mother and a father. They haven't been together since I was little—so I don't have parents. I got Mary and Fred."

Feather has fallen asleep in her car seat. Her little baby hands hold on to a stuffed duck with a really bent beak.

"Did you mind not having Mary and Fred together?"

Bobby laughs and waves to a man sitting on his porch smoking a pipe.

"Having Mary and Fred separately was more than any child could take. Mary is a photographer, and Fred is a chef. One was always dragging me off who knows where to get photo stories, and the other was always experimenting new recipes on me. I had an interesting childhood."

"Sounds great."

Bobby looks at me and smiles secretly. He always does it, and it makes me feel like I've missed something. "Isn't your life good?"

I say, "It was until a few weeks ago."

"Yeah, I see what you mean."

Bobby speeds up and flies by all the cornfields heading out of town.

When I was little, Mr. Calvin down the road used to threaten to put all us kids in the cornfields in the dark if we didn't stop running over his roses and peonies. We'd listen with our heads down and our hands folded in back of us. Then most of us would go home and have nightmares about corn monsters.

Mr. Calvin didn't have kids.

Pops said that to help me to understand why Mr. Calvin said the things he did to us. Pops always looked like he felt sorry for Mr. Calvin, childless and passing nightmares on to kids that weren't his.

Feather is still asleep as I carry her to the field with a blanket. Bobby carries his work things and the picnic basket. I lay Feather in the warm sun and watch her soft baby breathing. Bobby carries a ladder from behind the billboard, sets it up, climbs it, and takes off the huge tarp that has been covering his work.

Angela Johnson

Seconds later, I'm sitting in the morning sun looking at my dream . . . Bobby turns around once to me, smiles secretly again, then goes to work on the wings of a woman sitting on an airplane. . . .

ticket to heaven

Marley,

When you were a baby, I used to come into your room and sing to you. I'd sing from the radio. I'd make up songs and stay beside your crib until you would fall asleep. It got to the point where you wouldn't sleep until I sang.

Christine didn't think it was the best idea I ever had, 'cause I was the only one it worked for. What would happen, she said, if I wasn't able to be there for you some night? What if my work shift changed, or I had to be somewhere?

I kept telling myself that she was worrying for nothing. I'd be there forever . . .

When you write me about your friends, it helps me feel better that you have found a family outside of your family. I feel I've not left you alone.

My brother, your dad, could not love you more. The same goes for your mom.

Even though they love you—I think it's
time. I just decided to get a ticket to Heaven.
A ticket to you.
  Love,
  Jack

Shoogy was with me over by the park when I read the letter from Jack that said he had just bought a ticket to Heaven. . . .

Shoogy wonders why he isn't driving his truck or bringing Boy with him.

"I think he's speaking metaphorically."

Shoogy pushes her sunglasses up off her nose and sits with her back next to the park bench. There're hardly any kids in the park at all. It's quiet.

Shoogy leans toward me. "How do you feel, Marley?"

I look down the road leading past downtown then out of the village.

I say to myself, yeah—Marley, how do you feel? How do you feel?

Later that day, Pops says, "Do you mind that Jack is coming?"

We're sitting under the maple tree watching the sun go down.

"Who invited him, Pops?"

Pops watches the squirrels running up and down the picnic table.

"He invited himself. He wants to see you. He says it's time."

"Maybe he's wrong."

Pops puts his arm around me. "Maybe he's right."

When I was six, I got stuck in a snowdrift in our front yard. I remember I had painted a picture of some bears at school and I wanted to show my mom. I remember they were purple and orange and that I hadn't noticed that the snow was getting deeper as I ran slower and slower.

Finally, I was in the middle of the yard, stuck.

It seemed like I was stuck for an hour, but Momma said it was only a minute before she came out in a robe and Pop's tall fishing boots.

When I was warm and had shown my tear-streaked picture to Momma, she put in on the refrigerator and carried me into the living room. She sat me beside her on the couch and told me that I was okay and that she would always take care of me. That Pops would, too.

　　　　Angela Johnson

When he got home he dug out a trail from the middle of the yard. I watched him through the window from a chair.

After a while we laughed about me being trapped in the front yard. So close to home. I always laugh hardest at the story now, but I still don't walk through the front yard on snowy days.

Butchy's spinning 360s on the front sidewalk. He's moving to the music in his headphones, so I sit in the driveway and watch him do what he loves best. When he sees me watching him, he grins, but keeps on spinning. That's him.

I love Butchy.

He rolls over to me after a few minutes. "What, no applause?"

"I'm saving it up for your prime-time debut."

Butchy sits down beside me, and we roll his skateboard back and forth between us.

He says, "I thought you were supposed to be watching Bobby's kid today."

"Bobby took the day off to take Feather to the doctor for a checkup. It's not her favorite thing, and he said he liked me too much to put me through it."

"Yeah, guess you've been through enough the last few weeks."

heaven   133

"What? You worried about me?"

Butchy lowers his head and watches ants.

"I ain't worried. I just think about you some-times. I just think about . . . "

"How I'm not your blood sister."

Butchy lays down flat on his back in the drive-way and looks straight up. "It sucks."

I say, "Yeah, it does. Big time."

We both just let the idea that it sucks hang in the air. Wasn't much more to say about that part of it.

"Butchy, did you know Jack's coming here to meet me?"

Butchy looks at me like I just threw his skate-board in the river.

"He's not coming here?"

"Yeah, here."

"Marley, you aren't leaving with him or any-thing. I mean, you're ours. Not his."

"It's going to be okay. I mean—sooner or later."

Butchy jumps up and pulls me along with him. "Come on. Time for you to learn to ride."

Butchy runs in the house and brings out a hel-met. I didn't even know he had one. Momma just gave up on him after a while. He used to tie it around his waist.

Butchy runs along beside me for a couple of blocks on the sidewalk. I do mostly what he tells me except for a couple of times I fall on my face and butt. In a few minutes we're at the edge of town, heading downhill. A few seconds later, I'm flying on wheels past trees and houses and a couple of dogs barking.

After that I'm lying in a big yard just as the sprinkler comes on. Butchy is beside me.

"So that's what it's like?"

Butchy opens his mouth to drink some of the sprinkler water. "Oh, yeah, that's just what it's like."

"Some life, brother."

The water keeps coming down, and the people who own the house watch us from their living room window.

Butchy takes the helmet and puts it over his eyes. I listen to the tap, tap of the water on the helmet and Butchy's muffled voice.

"Yeah, it's some life."

heaven

$\mathcal{M}$omma said that it was destined we'd find Heaven. She said that postcard she found was supposed to be there. She believes in destiny and she says there isn't a damned thing any of us can do about it.

I believe I was destined to know the people I know and lose my mother in a car accident that wasn't supposed to happen. Jack was destined not to be able to stand any of it, and leave me.

Earlier today Shoogy, Bobby, and Feather showed up with a gallon of ice cream wearing cat masks left over from Halloween in July. We all sat in the backyard eating Rocky Road and collecting flies.

Nobody mentioned Jack. Bobby talked about going to the lake and getting a few buckets of sand for Feather. He didn't like the store-bought kind.

Shoogy said, "Let's go, cats." Hugged me and carried Feather to the car.

Bobby fed me a last spoonful of ice cream, then waved good-bye.

Mom, Pops, Butchy, and me sit in the living room and listen to the sounds of the summer. We try to talk to each other—to let each other know nothing is about to change.

Pops tells a joke.

We all laugh.

Mom tells a story about something that happened at work, and Butchy asks her if she thinks maybe some of the people in her office have too much free time. Mom says, "Definitely," and smiles.

It's like we're all strangers waiting for a bus at the station. Any minute somebody was going to ask somebody else to watch their iced tea so they could go to the bathroom.

A few minutes later, we're all laughing so hard at nothing that we don't hear the door slam in the driveway. And we don't see the man who looks like my dad and the dog who stands beside him watch us with a smile through the screen door.

There are 1,637 steps from my house to the Western Union in Heaven. I've walked by the playground, stores, and the coffee shop since I can remember. It was all old to me until I was suddenly pointing it all out to Jack, who quietly walked beside me with Boy.

I point out Ma's and say we should stop in—you can find anything you would ever need in there, and she wouldn't even mind having Boy come in.

Before we go in Jack looks through the window and asks, "They got Western Union?"

The question makes me smile.

Boy must already know the answer as he wags his tail and tries to nose his way in.

There's this sore part in my heart that isn't as aching as it was, so now I can smile about the Western Union. It hasn't been all that much time, either. I just don't hurt so much.

I don't want to hurt anymore. That's all.

I want to think about Momma and destiny, Pops, and how I got to see Jack's face all these years because of him.

My family is still just that—only the titles have been renamed. Butchy is still the boy I love, who rolls through life. Momma is still the one who digs and plants and does have hands that look like mine. And Pops is still the man who, when I close my eyes, I can see his smile.

I realized yesterday that a letter Jack sent last April was about me and Christine. We'd worn long dresses with sunflowers on them. He'd started telling me about my mother before I even knew she existed.

I watch Jack now as we all sit and talk in the back-yard, across from the river. Jack laughs with Pops and Momma shakes her head when she spots a new scar on Butchy's knees from his skateboard.

For a split second everything is so normal and warm. It's almost perfect, like the day I sat in the field with Bobby, Shoogy, and Feather. I don't feel like I could ever love any of these people more than I do in that one moment.

Shoogy would call it a Hallmark moment, then light up a cigarette and say, "Forget it," but only so I wouldn't know how she really felt. Bobby would say, "The moment was what it was."

They'd both be so right.

A story Jack told me about my mother . . .

Christine had been afraid of storms her whole life. When I was born she decided she needed to get over that fear. How would she ever make me brave if I saw her fear the wind and the lightning?

In the middle of the night when I was eight days old, a storm came blowing across the countryside. Jack remembered how Christine shook as she picked me up and carried me, wrapped in my blanket, out to the front porch. He watched from the window as she sang to me on the porch swing and faced the storm down.

In the end she went to sleep with me in her arms. Perfect.

I dreamed of Christine after Jack told me that story. I dreamed of sunflowers and talking vegetarian dogs too. I loved dreaming about Christine, and I want her to know that I love the river that winds by my house.

That I love the people who raised me by that river, and that I love the man who finally came back to tell me the stories I needed to hear from so long ago.

Even though some of the stories will hurt my heart and sometimes make me afraid of losing more of what I have; I want her to know that it's been a fine life, for a girl like me, in Heaven.

Angela Johnson

the first part last

For Elizabeth Acevedo
and the rest of the students
in the 1999–2000 sixth-grade class
at the Manhattan School for Children

part I

now

MY MOM SAYS that I didn't sleep through the night until I was eight years old. It didn't make any difference to her 'cause she was up too, listening to the city. She says she used to come into my room, sit cross-legged on the floor by my bed, and play with my Game Boy in the dark.

We never talked.

I guess I thought she needed to be there. And she must have thought her being there made everything all better for me.

Yeah.

I get it now. I really get it.

We didn't need to say it. We didn't have to look at each other or even let the other one know we saw each other in the glow of the Game Boy.

So last week when it looked like Feather prob-ably wasn't ever going to sleep through the night, I lay her on my stomach and breathed her in. My daughter is eleven days old.

And that sweet new baby smell . . . the smell of baby shampoo, formula, and my mom's per-fume. It made me cry like I hadn't since I was a little kid.

It scared the hell out of me. Then, when Feather moved on my stomach like one of those mechanical dolls in the store windows at Christmas, the tears dried up. Like that.

I thought about laying her in the middle of my bed and going off to find my old Game Boy, but I didn't.

Things have to change.

I've been thinking about it. Everything. And when Feather opens her eyes and looks up at me, I already know there's change. But I figure if the world were really right, humans would live life backward and do the first part last. They'd be all knowing in the beginning and innocent in the end.

Then everybody could end their life on their momma or daddy's stomach in a warm room, waiting for the soft morning light.

then

AND THIS IS how I turned sixteen. . . .

Skipped school with my running buddies, K-Boy and J. L., and went to Mineo's for a couple of slices. Hit a matinee and threw as much popcorn at each other as we ate. Then went to the top of the Empire State Building 'cause I never had before.

I said what everybody who'd ever been up there says.

"Everybody looks like ants."

Yeah, right. . . .

Later on that night my pops, Fred, made my favorite meal—cheese fries and ribs—at his restaurant. I caught the subway home and walked real slow 'cause I knew my mom had a big-ass cake for me when I got there, and I was still full. (In my family, special days mean nonstop food.)

I never had any cake though 'cause my girl-friend Nia was waiting on our stoop for me with a red balloon. Just sittin' there with a balloon, looking all lost. I'll never forget that look and how her voice shook when she said, "Bobby, I've got something to tell you."

Then she handed me the balloon.

now

I USED TO LAUGH when this old dude, "Just Frank" from the corner, used to ask me if I was being a "man." He never seemed to ask anybody else if they were being men; at least I never heard him. I laughed 'cause I didn't consider him much of one, a man, hangin' on the corner, drinking forties at ten in the morning. Hell, he was a joke. Always had been.

Two days after I brought Feather home, Just Frank got killed trying to save a girl in the neighborhood from being dragged into an alley by some nut job.

Didn't have any family. Didn't have any money, Just Frank. So the block got together to pay for his funeral, or the city was going to bury him in Potter's

Field. I went to his funeral at Zion AME, then walked home and held Feather for the rest of the night, wondering if I would be a man, a good man.

Feather sleeps like these kittens I saw once at a farm my summer camp went to. They were all curled up in an old crate, sleeping with paws on their brothers and sisters. Sleeping safe and with family.

I haven't been able to put her in her own bed at night, which used to be mine, since she came home from the hospital.

Mary, my mom, says I'm going to pay.

"Put that baby down, Bobby. I swear she's going to think the whole world is your face. She's going to be scared out of her mind when she turns about six and you haven't put her down long enough to see any of it."

Or . . .

"Bobby, you could have let your Aunt Victoria hold the baby for more than the thirty seconds it took for you to go to the bathroom. You are going to pay when she starts walking and won't let you out of her sight. You'll pay."

I wonder if somebody threatened her that one day I'd love her and want to be with her all the time. Some threat.

Angela Johnson

K-Boy and J. L. stand over Feather's bed, making faces and loud noises at her.

She screams.

They shake a rattle at her and tickle her feet.

She screams again.

I dive across my bed and put my Walkman on and watch them, laughing. "Yeah, you two are real good with her. If I was a baby I'd stop crying if a couple of tall men made scary faces at me and shook loud rattling sticks at my head."

J. L. picks her up like she's a football and walks her to the bedroom window. "Hey, man, my sister's got a baby, and I always get him to stop crying."

He starts to rock back and forth on his heels, humming something that I really can't hear. After about a minute she's stopped crying, and J. L. has slid to the floor with her. He keeps on humming. I see Feather's hands slowly rise then relax, and I know she's finally asleep. And in a few minutes J. L. is too.

K-Boy is standing at my desk, running his hand over a drawing that I did of Feather last night. "Nice."

"Thanks."

K-Boy takes his baseball cap off and his locks

the first part last

fall all over his face. He's mahogany and tall, and can't walk down the street without everybody staring at him. He's beautiful, but acts like he doesn't know it (Mom says). When we were ten he was almost six feet tall, and people who didn't know him treated him older. It would piss him off, people expecting teenage stuff from him when we were still jumping off swings at the playground.

K-Boy doesn't date. He just hangs out with girls. When I say stuff like this can happen to anybody (meaning a baby), even if you are just kicking it with some girl, K-Boy says no. It's different.

Everything is different if there ain't no love.

Didn't want to hear that then. And I guess I don't really want to hear it now. He's one of my best friends, but he's always saying stuff that makes me crazy.

Worse even is when he doesn't say anything at all. Then I got to wonder.

He keeps looking at the drawing of Feather.

"So. You going to keep her or what?"

I turn down my Walkman and look at him for a long time, wondering why he's my friend. "What do you mean am I going to keep her?"

He sits down on the bed beside me and grabs

the TV remote and starts watching a gardening show, muted. "It's a question, man."

"It's a stupid fucking question, K."

"Naw, Bobby, it's just a question. What's the problem?"

"Ain't no problem. No problem," I almost scream. Feather jumps in J. L.'s arms and his eyes snap open.

J. L. yawns. "What up?"

Nobody says anything. K-Boy turns the volume up on the TV, and I turn the volume up on my Walkman. J. L. nods off again.

A few minutes later this woman on TV is pointing at a mountain of dirt, and I say—like I'm talking to myself—"No doubt in my mind that I'm keeping her."

A few minutes after that, K-Boy has turned to the Weather Channel, but is looking across the room at J. L. and Feather. He says, "Too right you should keep her, man, too right."

then

FRED AND MARY SAT REAL STILL, and for a while I thought what I just told them about Nia being pregnant had turned both of them to stone.

It had been a long time since either of them ever agreed on anything.

So I waited. I waited to hear how they'd been talking to me for years about this. How we all talked about respect and responsibility. How Fred and me had taken the ferry out to Staten Island and talked about sex, to *and* from the island. And didn't we go together and get me condoms? What the hell about those pamphlets Mary put beside my bed about STDs and teenage pregnancy?

How did this happen? Where was my head? Where was my sense? What the hell were we going to do?

And then, not moving and still quiet, my pops just starts to cry.

now

My bones ache tired, but I'm wide awake.

I must be the only person up now. Even the city is quiet. Our neighborhood at least. I don't know what that means, except everyone in the world must have a new baby who kept them up most of the night and they've all passed out.

The rules.

If she hollers, she is mine.
If she needs to be changed, she is always mine.
In the dictionary next to "sitter," there is not a picture of Grandma.
It's time to grow up.
Too late, you're out of time. Be a grown-up.

I can hear Mary turn over in her sleep in the next room. She doesn't wake up 'cause Feather hasn't screamed yet. She whimpered herself awake, which means she only wants to be put in the bed beside me. No diaper change or formula needed. No big screaming fit. She only wants Daddy.

That scares the shit out of me.

Just me.

This little thing with the perfect face and hands doing nothing but counting on me. And me wanting nothing else but to run crying into my own mom's room and have her do the whole thing.

It's not going to happen, and my heart aches as I straighten out her hands and trace the delicate lines. Then kiss them. Her hands are translucent and warm. Baby hands. Warm, sweet-smelling baby hands. And all I can do is kiss them and pull her closer so she won't see my face and how scared I am.

When there's nothing you can do, do nothing.

But then I realize. I've done it. I know something. I know something about this little thing that is my baby. I know that she needs me. I know what she does when she just needs me.

No big screaming thing.

Just a whimper, then she only wants me.

Eight extra diapers.

Baby corn starch.

Baby wipes.

Three binkies (in case two get lost).

Four six-ounce bottles.

Three Onesies.

Three changes of outfits (she's barfing a lot).

One change of booties.

Diaper rash ointment.

Non-aspirin baby drops.

Two rattles.

One extra beanie.

Two cans of soy formula.

One can opener.

Two bottles of spring water.

And one cell phone all fit into the diaper bag K-Boy's mom gave to me two days after Feather was born. It all fits. Everything I need to get me from the Upper West Side to Bed Stuy for a whole day with Grandpa.

A few trains later and a nap (the motion just about puts me out right along with Feather) gets me to Pops.

When we get buzzed in and I'm holding her in

the carrier, going up in the 'vator, I think about the first time I came here, hand in hand with Fred, after him and Mary separated. I have to lean against the sides 'cause I could break down any minute. Just fall apart anytime before I get to my pop's apartment, which probably smells like chili-cheese fries. Just for me.

then

THEY ALWAYS LIKED ME.

Nia's parents always treated me good and trusted me. She told me they did. I didn't think much about it the whole time me and Nia used to be with each other.

I didn't think about it when we were on the subway to school, or hanging out at Mineo's, or skating in the park. What was I supposed to think about it, except it just was. It's good to be trusted, but you take it as it is. Nothing more. Nothing less.

Every wall in their loft is so white it almost hurts my eyes. Everything is straight lines and post-modern sculpture backlit. Stark white and so neat and clean you could probably make soup in the toilet.

I used to love this house 'cause I grew up in a place so different.

We have overstuffed pillows and Moroccan rugs and Jacob Lawrence prints all over the walls. Color and sound is what my parents were always about. Me and my brothers grew up in a loud house with jazz, Motown, or reggae music always playing in the background and something always on the stove.

Black-and-white pictures of my brothers and me in Africa, Spain, and Venezuela and Malaysia sit on every table, shelf, or furniture surface there is in the whole place. 'Cause even though Fred said we were poor, we never were too poor to travel, 'cause that made your spirit rich. He said.

To me, our house was crowded and noisy.

Nia lived in space and quiet.

When she comes through the Japanese doors that separate the bedrooms from the rest of the loft, Nia is backlit too. Just like a sculpture.

I see her like I never saw anybody before. Bathed in light like one of those angels in the paintings at the museums. So when she comes and sits by me, I almost holler when her hand covers mine and her silver and cowrie bracelet brushes against me.

She says, "They're coming in a minute. My

dad's on the phone and my mom . . ." She doesn't have to say anything else 'cause in a second her mom's backlit too, beside her father, and all I want to do is to get out of the light, back to the soft edges and color with something cooking on the stove.

They're cool and calm and sit hand in hand on the white couch with iron arms.

She smiles, her hair pulled back from her round face. I can just make out the circles under her eyes that she's covered with makeup.

He looks straight ahead like he's watching a movie outside the loft windows. It's like nothing that is about to be said or happen has that much to do with him.

He reminds me of my uncle L. C. when anybody starts talking about my cousin Sam who quit law school and went to be an aid worker in Africa. He just looks straight ahead and talks about the weather.

Oh, hell is all I can think when I know it's my turn to talk.

Yeah, Mr. Wilkins, I got your daughter pregnant.

Yeah, Mrs. Wilkins, I know that this is a tragedy 'cause you all expected more responsible behavior from us.

Oh, hell yeah, we know what's in store for us.

I can't tell you how upset my parents are, and the way my dad cried, and the way my mom wanted to slap me so hard she bit her lip till it bled down her chin.

No. I don't have any plans except shooting hoops with my partners at the rec center, and hanging out till we get bored and take in a movie. (Is this what you meant, Mr. Wilkins? Is this what you wanted me to say instead of I'm going to be the best father to me and Nia's baby that there ever was?)

But I say,

Yes, sir.

Yes, ma'am.

I don't know, ma'am.

I know, sir.

And on and on till it's like I'm almost blind from the cool white walls and the smile that hasn't left Nia's mom's face. 'Cause I know Nia told me she only does that when she's pissed and can't deal.

Then I know it's over when they both stand up and say something about wanting to speak to my parents, and Nia starts crying. I hate it that she cries first, before I do.

now

    I HOLD MY BABY in a waiting room that I used to sit in, way before I had her.

The nurse is the same one that has been smiling at me since my mom used to carry me in on her hip. The corkboard by the water fountain is still filled with pictures of kids, most laughing. The play area still has beat-up stuffed animals and cans of crayons pushed up against building blocks, dolls, and trucks.

I remember sitting here with Mary when I had a fever, needed to get stitches out, had to get a booster shot, fell into some poison ivy on vacation, and about a thousand other things that my pediatrician, Dr. Victor, took care of.

Now I'm sharing her with my daughter 'cause

I can still technically have a kid doctor for myself, even if I'm now technically a parent.

It's whacked, I know. And it didn't help that yesterday something happened that kind of messed me up.

I forgot Feather, and left her all alone.

K-Boy called me up to hit the nets a little and I said yeah. So I grabbed my basketball, zipped up my jacket, and headed out the front door.

Got all the way down the elevator.

I got all the way to the street door.

Then I was almost at the corner. . . .

She was still asleep as I crawled across the floor to her crib. Breathing that baby breath. Dreaming with baby eyes closed and sweet. And if she was older, just a little bit older, trusting that I'd be here for her.

I lay my basketball down and it rolled out the door into the hall toward Mary's room.

And I'd almost got all the way to the corner.

Dr. Victor picks Feather up and puts her on the baby scales. It's the first time I've seen her being weighed. She's a digital seven pounds and fifteen ounces.

"She's picking up weight, Bobby."

"Yeah, she drinks anything that you put in

front of her. I mean, she's doing good."

"She looks fantastic. And how are you? Tired?"

I adjust Feather's booties. Our downstairs neighbor, Coco Fernandez (I've always called her by her full name), made them out of angora (whatever that is). They're soft on the baby's feet.

Then Feather stretches and yawns like she'll never close her mouth.

I smile at Dr. Victor.

Damn, do I look tired? I want to say. Does it look like I've been up for three straight weeks with no breaks in between? I don't say it though. I just smile and try to keep from curling up in the baby carrier with the kid.

Won't do any good to complain about being tired. I already tried that with my mom. She couldn't have rolled her eyes any more than she did when I mentioned how tired I was and how maybe I wanted to go hang out awhile at the arcade.

"Your arcade days are over, brother." She laughed before she walked out the front door, mumbling something about going to develop some prints.

I smile up at Dr. Victor again. "I'm okay."

She looks at me for a minute then walks closer

Angela Johnson

and feels my neck. "I think you have swollen glands. Have you been feeling under the weather?"

I say again, "I'm okay."

Then I want to beg her for a note like I used to when I didn't want to do something and a sore knee or fever could get me out of it.

I want to say to this woman who'd always been nice to me and listened when I complained that damn it, I didn't feel good, I was so tired, I didn't know where I was going to lay down in a few hours, and by the way could she just write me a note and get me out of this?

It didn't have to be a long note.

It didn't have to tell anything about a medical condition.

It just had to get me out of staying awake all night, changing diapers every hour, and doing nothing except think of the yawning little thing in the white booties, whose baby carrier was all I wanted to be in.

I just want a note to get me out of it.

Just one note.

then

I SIT WITH NIA in a waiting room, with posters of pregnant women plastered everywhere. At least it seems like they're everywhere.

The Health Channel is starting to get on my nerves, talking about folic acid and good prenatal care, which is what we're here for. Damn, TV is everywhere. You can't even get away from it at the doctor's office. And I never thought I'd ever say that.

Nia's got her face in a magazine and hasn't looked up from it since she finished filling out the two-page questionnaire the nurse gave her.

I know she's trying to pretend she's not here.

Trying to pretend it never happened.

Trying to pretend we're just on some field trip

to the obstetrician's office. I know I'm doing a good job of denying just about everything that's been going on, to myself, so I figure she probably is too.

When I told Nia I wanted to go to her first appointment, she asked, "Why do you want to go?"

I said, "Shouldn't I go with you the first time?"

Nia starts reading her English book and not looking at me. "You don't have to, Bobby. I mean, I know how to get there by myself."

"Yeah, I know you know directions, Nia—I'm just trying to do the right thing. Mary says . . ."

Then it's the first time I see Nia really mad. It's like she wants to throw me across the room.

"So this isn't about what you really want to do. This is all about what your mom thinks you ought to do."

I try to explain, but she waves me off and walks out of study hall, and I don't have time to tell her all Mary said was that Nia's doctor was around the corner from where she had a shoot and maybe we could have lunch afterward.

Hell, I knew it wasn't going to be easy. Nothing ever is, anymore.

● ● ●

I don't remember everything. Just sitting in the doctor's office and looking at her skiing trophies on the shelves behind her.

I think she talked about how this whole thing should be a partnership and how Nia was going to count on me. She talked about Lamaze.

Nia said, "Uh, no. I *do* believe that all the pain medication in the world has to be used for this baby. I'm not into learning how to breathe. I do that just fine."

Then I stupidly say, "Maybe Lamaze would be better for the baby."

Nia stands up with one hand on her hip. She still only weighs about ninety pounds and isn't showing at all. But that doesn't mean she isn't full of attitude.

"Are you having this damned baby, Bobby?"

"No. Not even if I wanted to do it and spare you."

Nia chills and sits back down, grabbing my hand real tight before she looks at me with tears running down her face.

I look at the skiing trophies and think about how cool and windy it must be to go down the slopes, and how I always wanted to learn how to ski.

The doctor, I can't remember her name, says

Angela Johnson

something in a calm voice to Nia and doesn't look at me for the rest of the time we're there.

Nia keeps tapping her foot, and the doctor finally says that she needs to take Nia's blood pressure and get her ready for her exam.

"I don't have to be in there, do I?" I ask.

The doctor smiles like she feels bad for me, but not bad enough to leave the exam stuff out. But it turns out I'm wrong, because she sends me back to the waiting room to hang out till Nia is finished.

There I sit and listen to the health channel and dream that I have just sailed into the wind on skis, way into the wind, out of reach.

part II

now

THIS MUST BE IT.

This must be what made my mom's eyes narrow and nasty words come out of her mouth.

This must be what helped give my dad an ulcer and that look on his face that says—what next?

This must be it. The place where you really feel that it's all on you and you got a kid.

Feather spent last night in the hospital, with me sitting next to her bed all night long. I've had about twenty minutes' sleep in the last three days. Almost got locked in the toilet off the waiting room 'cause I was so sleepy I hallucinated being on the subway.

I got into a fight with a nurse.

Left my backpack in the taxi I came to the hospital in.

And before all of that, Feather threw up on the last clean jacket I had, and my mom is out of town and not answering her voice mail.

Half of Pop's kitchen staff called off and he's up to his ass . . .

She's sleeping now.

They say it was just a twenty-four-hour bug, but it scared the hell out of me when I went in to get her up from her nap and she was burning up. I could feel it through her bunny-rabbit sleeper, and it totally freaked me out. When I put the thermometer cone in her ear a few seconds later, it read 104.

It's twenty-four hours later, and we're home after hospital hell. I'm trying to get some sleep, but I'm too tired, if that makes sense.

Mom finally calls. "You okay, kid?"

She already knows Feather is okay. I'd been leaving voice mails every hour. I feel like a big old baby, but I can't help it, and when I finally hear her voice . . . I start crying like one. Only quiet so she won't know.

I manage a "Umm huh," and wish she'd hurry

up and finish shooting fruit and vegetables at farm markets and get the hell back to the city.

"I'll be back tomorrow," she says.

Then some leftover idiot that lives in me says, "Take your time. We're both just hangin' out now."

"Umm huh, Bobby. Remember to get Coco if you need anything."

I don't say what I want, which is for her to get home before I get an ulcer or start cussing strangers.

Instead, I wrap Feather up tight, lock the door behind me, and thirty seconds later I'm down the iron fire stairs and at Coco's door.

"Come in if you're good looking," she yells. Then, "Come in even if you're not. I'll give you a makeover."

I walk into a powder blue apartment with squishy dark blue carpet, and pictures of her kids and grandkids everywhere. Bluegrass is playing on the stereo.

Coco is a fiddle player in a bluegrass band.

She's known me forever, and comes over and starts kissing Feather before she takes her out of my arms.

"I got your message," she says, smiling so her whole face scrunches up. She's got some sort of twenty-colored scarf tying all her dark hair up, and she's wearing one of her hundred "I Luv NY" shirts with sweatpants. I've been taller than her my whole life, and Feather probably weighs more than her. They are the same caramel color, though.

"I figured I'd missed you." I yawn.

"Yeah. We had a gig at this revival in the Village. I hadn't seen a lot of those people since the seventies."

I sit down and watch the fish in Coco's aquarium swim back and forth.

The next thing I know, it's six hours later and Feather is asleep beside me on Coco's couch.

I've got about three hours before school starts.

Feather wakes up as I carry her up the fire stairs and unlock the door to our apartment.

When I walk past my mom's room, I miss her.

I walk to my room, put Feather in her crib, which pisses her off and makes her scream, and then I look around my room and miss me.

then

K-BOY AND J. L. LEAN AGAINST THE WALL of the West Side Rec Center and don't say anything. Then they shift their stance and look across the street while three girls cross it, talking loud and laughing. And when the girls almost get hit by a taxi, they flip the driver off and keep on walking.

J. L. laughs and sucks down the bottle of water he pulled out of his backpack a minute ago.

I keep waiting.

I keep waiting for them to say anything about what I just told them. For the first time I don't know what they'll say. I know it's stupid, but I'm more afraid of what they'll say about Nia being pregnant than I was about my parents.

J. L. is the first to open his mouth.

"Yo, Bobby. I need some money for a phone call. You got change on you?"

And I'm thinking, I just told him my girl is having a baby and all he wants to do is make a phone call.

I reach into my pocket and K-Boy starts laughing.

"What the hell is so funny?" I yell at him 'cause both of them are seriously starting to get on my nerves. What the hell, anyway?

K-Boy stops laughing, but he really doesn't want to.

J. L. leans back against the Center again. "Hey, Bro, I was just going to make a call for you to 1-800-ISTUPID."

K-Boy looks sorry for me and starts shaking his head. I don't know what I expected. I would have probably said the same thing.

We all talked about this. We said only stupid people would let it get to this. 'Cause there is birth control. Lots of it.

My mom always kept a big basket of rubbers underneath the bathroom sink for my brothers, and when they both left—just me. She said she didn't want to have to talk about it every time she thought about it.

So there they were.

K-Boy and J. L. got most of their supplies from me.

J. L. 'cause he was always broke and K-Boy 'cause his moms almost lost her mind when she found a pack of condoms underneath his bed.

She didn't want to hear he was being safe. She just wanted him not to do it. Didn't want to ever know that he thought about sex, had sex, or hung out with people who might be having sex too.

"What can I say?" K-Boy shrugged.

"What do you want us to say?" J. L. said, looking kind of sorry he'd been an asshole a few minutes ago.

"Nothing," I say, and turn to watch the little kids running around the rec center playground. And I'm thinking while I'm watching how in three or four years my kid's going to be out there screaming and falling down with the rest of them.

J. L. picks his backpack off the ground and starts walking off. He doesn't turn around for almost a block. When he finally does, K-Boy nods to him, and I act like I don't even see him.

"Shit. Never seen J. L. like that," K-Boy says.

We start walking down Columbus and I don't hear the people or cars, and it's rush hour. Everything is a blur, and the only thing I see is my

Angela Johnson

feet in hiking boots and K-Boy in tennis shoes.

K-Boy says, "Shit," again.

"Yeah," I say. "That's pretty much where I'm at."

K-Boy brushes against my shoulder trying to dodge two kids on Rollerblades.

"Nia okay? 'Cause I know she is seriously into the books. . . ."

"She's out of it. Last time I talked to her all she could do is get out a few words. Mostly she just cries."

"I feel you, man. I mean I wouldn't want to be ya, but I feel you."

"Hell, I don't want to be me either."

Two girls pass by us and stare at K-Boy. I mean they stop in the middle of the sidewalk and stare. He smiles back.

I grab him by the arm. "Uh huh, they are so fine, but not today."

K-Boy laughs, looks at me, and we keep on walking.

"So—she keeping it or what?"

I say, "I don't know. She doesn't want to talk about it. She doesn't say yes. She doesn't say no."

"Bobby, what do you want her to do?"

My stomach is hurting by the time that question is out of his mouth and into the air. I don't say; it's not up to me. I don't say; whatever I want, I can't say. My dad already told me now was the time to shut my mouth. What Nia wants is what it's all about.

No pressure.

A minute later I'm puking in front of a flower shop and K-Boy is telling the owner to stop screaming at me, grow a heart, and get out of my face.

"Shit," I say.

K-Boy takes a T-shirt out of his backpack so I can wipe off my jacket. We walk on and K doesn't stop at his turnoff, but walks me the five blocks to my apartment, watches me go in, then turns and heads home.

I sit on the stairs to catch my breath before I climb up to my floor.

Angela Johnson

now

I CAN HARDLY KEEP MY EYES OPEN in Brit Lit. I got so much drool on my arm I can't even try to wipe it on my shirt. I seriously need a tissue or a paper towel.

I was up all night with Feather, who thinks two in the morning is party time. She just smiles, though, unless you try to put her down, then she screams like it's the end of the world.

I walked her.

I played music for her. She likes dance music and can't stand the Bach for Babies my aunt bought her.

When the music stopped she screamed or twisted herself up in a bunch so tight it even made me feel cranky. So I talked to her. Told her about what was going on.

It's cool when I talk to her. I could be saying anything. I could be talking about basketball or my bad grades in math.

I could be telling her how she looks like her mom. And asking if she remembers her. It hasn't been that long ago.

As long as my mouth is moving, she's happy. As long as sound is coming out of it, the whole world is just fine for my caramel, sweet-faced, big-eyed baby; who's killing me, and keeping me so tired I can't keep my eyes open.

So in the end I'm busted by Mr. Philips, my Brit Lit teacher.

When the bell rings, he points to me and mouths, "Stay put."

I do.

And this is how it goes.

"I hear you're a father."

I rub the sleep out of my eyes, and for the first time, really the first time, notice that he's one of the tallest men I've ever met. What made him want to be a teacher? Hell, he was taller than most pro basketball players.

Why was he here? Teaching kids like me and kids who weren't like me but must be just as bad?

Angela Johnson

I keep rubbing my eyes 'cause it keeps me from having to talk. At least it seems that way to me. I'm sick of talking. I've been talking to a baby all night long and into the morning.

I notice his khakis and then his blue polo shirt. Then I look at the way the light bounces off his almost bald head. His head isn't shiny though 'cause he's got hair growing in. Maybe he's growing it back.

Hell. Why do I care? I think I might be going crazy from lack of sleep.

"I said, I heard you're a father."

Then I wake up. "Yeah, I got a baby."

"The mother go to this school?"

"She used to," I say.

He smiles like one of the social workers I had to talk to.

"Did she transfer to another school?"

I look at his shoes. Loafers. What's that about anyway?

"No."

"She helping you out? I mean, I heard that the baby is living with you."

I try the eye rubbing thing again and think how I'm going to get him out of my business. Shit! People in this school talk too much. Everybody's always got so much to say, and never really says anything that's worth talking about.

He probably drives a Jeep, and his girlfriend and him have been engaged for two years. They probably laugh at the same jokes and plan to have two kids and go to Disney in the summer.

What the hell does he know?

"Yeah, my kid lives with me."

"Well, I hope you're getting help."

Then he just leaves.

I'm thinking he's going to tell me how he'll give me a break on my grades or something. Something. But that ain't happening.

He just hopes I'm getting help.

I rub my eyes again and hope my shirt dries from all the spit on it and remember I have to stop by the store on the way home from school to pick up some more formula.

I have to change twice on the subway to get to the baby-sitter in Brooklyn to pick up Feather.

Jackie's poodle keeps barking at me. The stupid dog's known me for years and still keeps acting like it's never seen me.

What's the problem?

I walk into the toy-covered living room and remember playing in it when I was little. Nothing's changed. Nothing.

Angela Johnson

I can almost taste the toasted cheese sandwiches and tomato soup that I couldn't get enough of.

I remember the box of play clothes and the corner off the dining room where me and Paco Morales painted the carpet polka-dot.

Jackie looks the same.

Laughs the same, shaking when she laughs and tossing her beaded braids in back of her when she puts her hands on her hips to tell one of the parents that she needs to give her baby more green vegetables to make him regular.

She's probably talked the same way to parents for thirty years.

She probably talked to my own mom that way. Everybody listened.

So when she says, "Boy, you look old and tired," I sit on the floor like I used to and think about how easy it was when me and Paco thought the carpet needed spots. She puts Feather in my arms and leans down close to me, braids clicking with beads, and says, "But it'll change for sure. I know it will. I just know."

I want to ask her how she knows, but I'm too tired, so all I can do is hold my baby and think about the two changes we have to make to get home.

then

NIA'S SCARFING DOWN TACOS like she hasn't eaten in a week. I know she ate two hours ago, because I was the one that picked up the pineapple-and-pepperoni pizza for her at Mineo's.

"It'll be cold by the time I get it to you," I said, screaming over the sound of jackhammers and taxis blowing down Broadway.

"That's okay. What do you think stoves are for? I don't mind cooking it a few more minutes."

"You sure you want a slice this early in the morning? I don't even know if they fire the oven up this early."

"Bobby, it's a pizza shop."

"Yeah, but this early they usually only serve pastries and espresso."

I'm not gonna get out of this. She wants a pizza at ten o'clock on a Saturday morning, and the quiet on the other end of the phone means she's as serious as a heart attack.

I head toward Mineo's.

And all I'm wishing is that Nia's parents didn't live in Chelsea 'cause if she was gonna get a jones for Mineo's on the Upper West Side I was going to be hopping a lot of buses.

Now she's sitting on the floor against the dining room wall, stuffing more tacos down her throat. She looks tired. And she looks good.

Real good.

She's all in black. V-neck sweater, black pants, and some sort of ruffle black thing that pulls her curly brown hair up in a ponytail.

When she takes a breather from eating, she brings her feet up, sits cross-legged, and plays with a silver toe ring on her left foot. She smiles at me sitting across from her with my back against the couch.

I say, "Feel better now?"

She nods her head, crawls across all the taco papers and salsa containers, and curls up around me. She smells like baby shampoo and hot sauce.

In a few minutes we're wrapped around each

other on the floor. She smells sweet and her mouth is tangy, then sweet, then tangy again.

All I can think is that I want her more than anything. I want her more than I've ever wanted anything, ever.

She pulls my T-shirt over my head and kisses me so soft on my neck. She's everything that I ever thought I wanted when I take her sweater off and kiss all the soft places, the warm places, down to her stomach. . . .

I stay there for a long time, warming my face on her swollen belly. She sighs and holds my head. I close my eyes and want to stay there.

"Is it too early for the baby to move?"

She giggles. "Yeah, I think so."

I look over at all the taco wrappers and the pizza box.

"I guess it's not too early for it to eat like a starving pig though."

She giggles again.

Kissing her belly is like eating ice cream. I can't stop. I don't want to stop. So I don't.

She starts to shiver and I watch her arms and stomach get goose bumps on them, so I wrap myself tighter around her.

I whisper, "Is it okay? I mean, will it hurt the baby if we do it?"

Angela Johnson

She sits up against the couch and smiles.

"No. I got all these pamphlets and things from the doctor. All of them say it's okay, just use common sense."

I figure we hadn't used too much common sense lately, or she wouldn't be pregnant.

"My parents won't be home until tonight. We've got a long time."

I pull her to me then lift her up off the floor.

We step on the pizza box as we head toward her room. I'm glad we have a long time. I'm glad.

now

I SHOULD HAVE SCOPED how the day was going when Feather puked on me just as I picked her up out of her crib this morning.

But I didn't hear it or see it.

Fred always talks about the signs being there. He says he can tell in the morning if a waiter is going to quit or some delivery isn't going to come. The only way to change something is to pay attention to the signs.

But K-Boy says it doesn't matter what you do, what's gonna go down is already set. Try to change something—be damned. Don't try to change it—be damned just as much.

So I should have just called in sick to school

and watched the purple dinosaur all day long with the baby.

I should have just hid.

But in the end there was probably nothing I could do about anything anyway. If you look at it that way I guess it makes what goes down, go down easier.

And 'cause I was going to be late getting Feather to the sitter, I knocked on Coco's door.

'Cause I had to give Feather a bath it made everything late. I'd already been called into the guidance counselor's office twice.

She smiled a lot and asked if everything was running smooth. Was fatherhood what I thought it would be? Was the responsibility of a baby getting to be too much? Was my mother helping? My father? The baby's other grandparents?

I fell asleep in her warm office and can't remember what lie I answered to most of her questions.

I wasn't up for that today.

I didn't think I was ever gonna be up to that any day. Never talked to so many adults in my whole life. It was getting right down to my last nerve.

Hell, I didn't have any nerves left.

So I did what my mom asked me not to do. I took the easy way out and asked Coco to do me a favor.

She came to the door in a star-burst caftan, her hair tied up in braids and a cup of coffee in her hand. "Hey, kid."

I carried Feather in, strapped in her carrier. Anybody would have wanted to keep her, dressed up cute in her pink teddy bear snowsuit.

Coco took the carrier from me and smiled.

All of a sudden my backpack is feeling heavy and it's all I can do not to fall on my knees to the soft carpet.

Coco says, "Running late? You need I should keep the little mouse pie?"

"Yeah, could you? I mean I wouldn't ask if the morning wasn't already shot, and my mom hadn't left about five this morning with every camera she had in the world to get some sunrise shots of the city."

"Hmmm." Coco hums.

"And she hasn't got back yet—Feather puking and it taking forever to get her to take a bottle."

I must have looked whacked 'cause Coco started unbuckling Feather while I held her coffee.

"Go to school, Bobby. I got her."

I could've cried and hugged Coco all at the same time but I just leaned over, kissed Feather, and told Coco I'd see her after school and what channel the purple dinosaur was on. She looked at me like I was crazy.

I should have hung with the first idea. Should have called off school and watched the big lizard with the kid all day.

then

J. L. RUNS TO THE DOOR to make sure what we hear out in the hall isn't going to get us kicked out of school for three days.

It's just some kid late for class.

And I don't even want to ask J. L. how he'd gotten the keys to Nelson's room. It's never good to know too much about what J. L. has in the back of his head. But it's cool 'cause it's usually kickin'.

Something stupid.

Something dumb.

Always funny.

Today we're turning everything in Nelson's room upside down. Desks, chairs, posters, garbage cans, whatever.

Just about the time we get to the desks, J. L. starts laughing and can't stop. *He's laughing so hard you can hear him in the hall,* I thought.

"Shut up, man. You're gonna get us busted."

J. L. pulls on his baseball cap and keeps laughing.

"Man, this is so stupid—what we're doing. It's so stupid I can't help it. . . ."

Then he starts laughing so hard he ends up on the floor.

I look at him curled up on the floor, gasping, then I look around the room and start laughing too. This is about the dumbest thing we ever did. But it feels good after the last couple of months with everything being so heavy with Nia and all.

We get out without getting caught, lock the room up, and push the extra set of keys back underneath the door. We walk to the third floor, get chips out of the machine, and head back to study group.

Never get to see how Nelson looks or how everybody laughs when they see the room 'cause five minutes after we're sitting back in group, the teacher gives me a note to say I'm excused.

Nia got real sick and was rushed to the hospital. And when I think the kid is here already, I remember she's only a few months pregnant.

I sit on the subway a few minutes later thinking, yeah, life is stupid.

Nia's sleeping when I get to the hospital.

I sit at the foot of her bed and rub her feet 'cause I know the only thing she likes more is having her back massaged. But I can't do that now.

The white sheet is curving around her stomach and I don't notice at first that the sheet is moving a little. I figure she's waking up, but when it does it again and her eyes are still closed, I know.

It's like a dream when I move my hands from her feet, up her legs and hips to her belly, and it kicks me.

I put my head on her stomach and it's like I'm stoned, and don't wake up till the nurse comes in to take Nia's temperature. I leave Nia sleeping.

Don't remember anything except how I walked about fifty blocks and it only seemed to take a few minutes to get home.

Angela Johnson

now

I LEAVE COCO'S APARTMENT and think how easy it would be if every morning fifty steps would get Feather to her baby-sitter.

Hell, that's living in a dream.

But all of a sudden I have time that I don't usually have.

No school for about an hour and a half.

And there's that thing I haven't done in a long time. Forgot that it used to juice me to do it, and now I need to do it, like yesterday.

I run back upstairs and put about four cans in my backpack before I go to Mineo's for a coffee and some kind of donut so full of sugar it almost blows my head off.

I'm feeling good.

Haven't felt this let loose in a while, and I almost can't stand it. Found this great wall a few weeks ago off the Ave. And it's time to do some tagging.

I cut through the parking lot and through the playground, an alley, and over and down a wall to get where I need to be. Perfect.

Everything is clean brown brick, and off in the shadows of some brownstones.

Where the hell did this wall come from anyway? It's just standing here in the middle of the city, not connected to anything or holding anything up. It's just been waiting for me.

I sit down against it. Feel the bricks and let the cool settle in me. I'm feeling colors and seeing things now that I'm against the wall.

There's flashes of me and K-Boy climbing up a fire escape and tying our kites to a clothesline and watching them all day.

After that, me and J. L. are at the Museum of Natural History in the shadows, looking at million-year-old rocks, and blowing bubbles on the front stairs.

Then I'm in Jamaica on a beach with my brothers burying me in the sand. My mom's snapping pictures of us while Fred keeps worrying that they'll get sand in my eyes.

In a few minutes my face is wet.

Tears are still pouring out when I start spraying the clean brick.

The tears are still coming when I start from the beginning and go to now.

I'm always the pale ghost boy between everybody. Floating in and out of the paintings. One minute I'm just getting J. L.'s face right.

I'm the pale white ghost boy beside the brown girl who is always looking away. Sometimes in the picture, my brothers show up, make themselves known, then leave the painting again.

Like in real life.

Finally it's just me and the thing in the baby carrier who doesn't have a face for a long time. There are bottles and boxes of diapers, hospitals, and social workers. There's the baby with no face and the ghost boy at the courts.

Then they're at the arcade and the bodega by K-Boy's house. The carrier sails through the painting, following the ghost boy. Pretty soon he's going to have to look inside the carrier and make up a face for the kid if it's gonna be following him all over the damned place anyway.

He's going to have to see it.

I spray black.

Then red, mixed with some blue.

The boy's got to be paler. But no, maybe just some green all around him. Maybe just some more green.

I'm losing wall now.

It's all got to come to an end soon. I'm going to have to find the kid's face. It's going to be hard now 'cause I'm out of breath and running out of color in the cans.

I'm almost empty.

But I got to find the baby's face.

And when I feel a hand on my shoulder, at first I think it's some kind of savior coming along to help me out. Help me find it's face.

Then I notice it's kind of dark and it isn't just dark from the building's shadows.

I've been here all day. Way past school, and near the night.

I get about two seconds of relief until the savior turns out to have a uniform and a gun, and I'm sitting in the back of the radio car all the way to the station.

Angela Johnson

part III

then

So here's a good day.

We'll call it a fairy tale day.

Once upon a time, really right now, there was this hero (I always wanted to be one) who lived in the city. He was born in the city, loved the city, and never ever wanted to be anywhere else but the city.

He loved the feel of it. The way you got juiced when you walked down the sidewalk and everybody was out.

He loved the smell of it. Pizza on one corner, falafel and French pastries on the next. Standing in front of the Chinese restaurant, wondering if you want soup or if you should jump a train to that Jamaican place that K-Boy got kicked out of.

He loved the sounds that woke him in the morning and put him to sleep at night. And when he left the city and the noise to go someplace else—another country or town—he missed it.

Couldn't sleep without the ambulance noises and people calling to each other in the street who are just getting back from the clubs.

He couldn't help but get used to the delivery trucks that pulled up early for the restaurants in the neighborhood and the jackhammers and horns. He loved the sounds the kids made running to the subway, and cabs blowing by and screeching to a stop.

Now, 'cause this is a fairy tale, it's important to have some sort of monster, but I've decided not to include him in the story. Decided that because this was a perfect day, we didn't need him along to screw up the magical kingdom and run crazy through the streets, breathing fire and knocking down pizza joints and hot dog stands.

Whatever the monster is, it has to understand that the kid has got friends who hang out with him and usually got his back, and some days it just ain't worth it.

I mean even in a fairy tale the friends could be asses and stuff, give the hero a hard time when he gets stupid or something, but they're there. When everything gets real hard. Right there.

Now. The damsel.

Definitely in distress.

Sitting in a castle in Chelsea.

The hero is there to rescue her from her royal relatives who aren't evil, but lately have been trying to do a close imitation of it.

No white horse here.

Got a pass for the subway though.

The hero is buzzed up to the castle with his buddies waiting outside. The damsel's parents are at friends' having brunch and she's all alone. No mama dragon at the gate. No three deeds to do in order to open it up.

The damsel is all in black, dark glasses, and a smile 'cause she doesn't have to stay in her royal bedchambers anymore. The royal doctors just said not too much stress and watch the blood pressure.

The hero rides down the elevator with the damsel to meet his buddies on the street to go into the city kingdom and have the best time.

They go to the magical forest and watch the skaters, skateboarders, and other subjects laughing, talking, reading, eating, kissing, hugging, screaming. It's perfect that the magical forest runs right through the kingdom.

Angela Johnson

There's even a castle in the magical forest. They sit around the castle, eating popcorn, soda, and franks. The hero is happy with the damsel, who glows when the sun hits her curly hair and smiling face.

The buddies spend most of the time cracking on people and laughing at just about everything that moves. They each run around the magical forest, getting different foods for the damsel.

One even brings back a rock he swears looks like the super in his building.

He gives it to the damsel, saying, "Hey, girl, it's not Elvis, but you could keep it on top of some papers and think of my super."

The damsel says, "I don't know your super."

"So?"

"Shouldn't you keep it?"

"I don't want it."

The damsel eats another pretzel and laughs, "But it looks like your super."

The running buddy says, "Yeah, but I don't like our super."

So the damsel says, "We shouldn't be taking rocks out of the park anyway," and throws it across the grass into the trees. I forgot that the damsel has some arm.

The damsel sits back down and leans against

the hero. She's asleep in one minute. The hero covers her with his jacket.

And because this is a fairy tale, the hero and his running buddies lay back and talk about battles that they've won and places that they've seen.

There have been a lot of dragons.

More damsels for some than others.

They swam a lot of moats and ate many feasts. And mostly they've all done it together, 'cause a long time ago in the kingdom they became blood brothers, and that's what blood brothers do. Especially in a big kingdom like this one, on a good day that could be like a fairy tale.

Angela Johnson

now

I GOTTA CATCH A BREAK.

The cop who brings me in is on the phone, and looking through some file like she's got nothing to do but slowly look through paper.

We walk up tiled stairs past gray walls to a squad room.

She points to a chair and says, "Sit, kid."

I sit.

And when I look at the clock over the window facing a brick wall, I feel my stomach turning over. 7:30 P.M. Coco must be buggin' with my mom beside her, burning up every phone on the island.

By now my dad—who always thinks that way anyway—is imagining me cold in a Dumpster. It started as a real bad dream, but it's turning into a freakin' nightmare.

Then somebody is talking about night court and putting me in a holding cell till they get a hold of a parent.

All I'm thinking about in the gray cell, nasty 'cause I can tell somebody was sick a minute ago, is my baby. And how if I'm lucky I won't be murdered by her grandma if I get out of here in maybe—ever.

On the other side of things, I'm pretty scared about being dragged out of the station and being treated like I had been doing something dangerous and insane.

Doesn't Five-0 have anything to do besides bust underage artists? I want to ask, but I'm not talking 'cause that's what everybody says you should do.

Anyway, the cops can't do anything as bad to me as my mom can, and she never has to put a hand on me. All she has to do is walk around with a mom badge and her arms folded up serious tight in front of her.

Busted.

Mom lives by the rules and doesn't take bullshit—which is what skipping school, getting arrested for street art, and leaving Feather with Coco is.

Angela Johnson

Since both of Mom's parents were serious alcoholics, she can't take the crazy stuff. So we were dragged to meetings in church basements and school cafeterias. I guess she wanted to be ready when me and my brothers were on the street with forties in paper bags.

My one phone call is to my dad. I know he'll be in the restaurant, and he won't be nasty mad like my mom probably will. At least I think he won't.

8:45 P.M.

It's been fourteen hours since I dropped my baby off at Coco's house and I stepped into this. So I'm waiting for whoever to come get me so I can see just how big everything's been nuked.

He doesn't say anything to me in the station, but when we get into the cab he says, "Have you eaten?"

"No," I say, and try to look real interested in the raindrops on the taxi window.

"Do we need to stop by someplace and pick up takeout?"

"I'm not hungry, Dad," I whine.

"When was the last time you ate, anyway?" he says, looking real concerned, like he just picked me up from a hospital 'cause I passed out from lack of lunch, instead of the police station.

It's the way he deals.

Mom says if they could have just eaten the food he cooked twenty-four seven, and not had to deal with each other any other way, they'd still be married.

Whatever.

It's raining hard now.

"You left a mess at home, Bobby."

I feel like I'm going to throw up, again.

"You didn't call the sitter in Brooklyn to tell her you weren't going to show, so she got nervous. I guess there's about twenty messages from her."

"God."

"And since Coco couldn't get you on your cell . . . You know I got it for you so anyone who had the baby could stay in touch with you."

"I know, Dad. I know. I just didn't think about it being off."

He looks sad for me, but I must have been hallucinating 'cause the next second he's saying, "You seriously messed it up today. Coco couldn't get your mom, and I was out of the restaurant most of the day. She was on the verge of calling the cops."

"Shit," I say, then sink down lower in the seat

Angela Johnson

when I can feel my dad's eyes shooting holes through me in the dark taxi. "Sorry."

"There's going to be a whole lot of apologizing going on tonight, kid."

"Yeah, I guess so. All I want now is to go home, curl up in my bed, and sleep for two days."

Fred turns away from me.

"There'll be no sleep for you. There's ten pounds of I need my daddy, a pissed-off mother, and a disappointed neighbor waiting at home. You ready to deal?"

I say, "I guess," and sink farther into the seat.

My dad's shoulders come to the same part of the seat as mine, but I got longer legs. His face is kind and he's got laugh lines that don't crinkle like they used to. I guess I've taken a lot of his smile away.

And right now, besides a gurgling stomach and the look I know my mom is going to give me along with the hell, I feel worse because I'm taking my dad's smile and probably some more things he'll never talk about.

The taxi pulls up to the apartment. I look up to the third-floor window and see my mom's outline in the window. She's holding Feather.

My dad doesn't go in with me.

I think about how Feather is probably asleep

and will wake back up in two hours, and how she loves to be held. I climb the stairs and think about holding her, or maybe I'm really thinking about just holding on to her.

Angela Johnson

then

K-Boy starts laughing in his sleep, then almost kicks himself awake. Something in his dreams is so funny he even shakes his head from side to side and acts like he's about to hold on to his stomach.

He's always laughed in his sleep, where J. L. doesn't move at all. He's in the same place from the time he goes to sleep till he wakes up in the morning.

I know how they sleep 'cause we used to nap together at preschool. We got in trouble more than we slept. Everybody is sleeping now, though.

We'd all stayed up late, first hangin' out at Mineo's till he'd kicked us out and told us to find a home or something. Then we'd gone up on the roof of K-Boy's building to play some new CDs he'd just got, till one of his neighbors started screaming that she was gonna call a cop if we didn't turn it down.

We didn't, till she came up to the roof.

She was seriously scary, so we left to hang out at my house 'cause my mom was gone for the night. We could eat most of the stuff in the icebox, then order Thai food if we were still hungry.

I still felt full and had slept like a pig when I finally did sleep, and now the phone's ringing.

"Hello," I say, and knock K-Boy's foot out of the way so I can get a bottle of water that rolled under my bed.

Nia's sleepy voice is on the other end.

"It's me. What did you do last night?"

"Hung with K-Boy and J. L."

She starts to eat something while she's talking. Then she burps real loud.

"Jeez, Nia. Did you get any on you?"

"Yeah, I did. If you were big as a house and had something living inside you, you'd burp out of control and make other disgusting noises too."

"Thanks for sharing that with me."

"I'd like to really share the whole damned

experience with you. How about the swollen ankles, or the aching back?"

"No, thanks."

She's getting started, I can tell, 'cause she takes a deep breath.

"How about the hemorrhoids or the constant peeing? How about how normal smells can make you sick or the way I can fall asleep in the middle of a sentence?"

I say, "Naw, that's okay." But I know it's not a joke anymore 'cause I can hear her voice getting high. It's like I can almost see her jangling the phone cord and shaking her leg.

I leave my room and go out in the hall. By the time I'm leaning against the wall outside of my mom's bedroom, Nia's crying. She does it so much now, but I'm still not used to it.

I whisper, "Sorry, Nia. I'm sorry everything is so messed up. I didn't mean for this to happen."

"Neither did I."

"I know it was my fault."

Nothing.

"I can 'fess to it. I was stupid."

I start to think that she's hung up the phone. I hear J. L. and K-Boy waking up in my room. My stereo comes on too loud for ten o'clock on a Sunday morning.

"Turn it down, man," I holler out to whoever turned it on in the first place. They turn it down.

"Nia."

Nothing.

"Nia."

Her voice is soft and low. "My parents are talking about sending me to my grandma's house in Georgia. They say I wouldn't be under so much stress there."

I want to cry. I want to cry a whole lot these days, and sometimes I do, and this makes me crazy.

"The doctor says my blood pressure is still too high. School and everything. They're talking about a tutor."

"In New York or Georgia?"

"Wherever, Bobby."

K-Boy must have seen someone out on the street 'cause I hear the window going up and him laughing and calling to somebody downstairs.

Nothing's changed and everything has. Whoever K-Boy called out to is doing the same ole same ole. I hear J. L. up, complaining about what's for breakfast. But Nia is talking about going. And even if she's not going, she's talking about it all being different.

"Bobby."

Angela Johnson

"Yeah."

"Do you want me to go?"

The music is getting loud slowly. K-Boy takes off the rap he started with and puts on some techno. I feel better when I say to Nia, "Don't go, okay? Don't leave."

She says, "Can we go out for pizza later? You can have anchovies on yours if you want."

"Cool with me."

"Cool with me too, Bobby. I'll see you later."

I walk into the kitchen to make breakfast, and even though nothing's changed yet, I miss her already.

now

HER EYES ARE THE CLEAREST EYES I've ever seen.

Sometimes she looks at me like she knows me. Like she's known me forever, and everything I ever thought, too. It's scary how she looks at me.

And she's so new. Been on the planet for only a few months. I been thinking about it a whole lot lately. I feel old.

I feel old when I wake up at three thirty in the morning and change her diaper, then change it again when she pees right after I put her sleeper back on.

I feel old when I stroll her into Mineo's, park her by my table while I eat a few slices and catch up on the comics I haven't read in weeks.

I really feel old when I'm holding her on the subway and some lady tells me what a good brother I am and how I'm so good with her. I feel stooped over then. You'd think I'd feel young.

For that one time on the way home I could pretend my baby is my sister. I could smile at the lady and say:

"Yeah, she's easy to deal with, my sister."

"She looks just like me and my brothers."

"I like to help my mom with her."

Even if I'm feeling old when this stuff happens I just change her diaper, put my food down and hold her when she cries, and tell the woman on the train that she's mine.

Afterward I always kiss her, my baby, and look into her clear eyes that know everything about me, and want me to be her daddy anyway.

then

"YOU GONNA DANCE, Bobby?"

"Yeah, in a minute."

My head's hurting. Never got a damned headache from music before. Too, too loud. The music is making the walls jump. I guess it's a good party.

Jess's parents are out of town for the weekend and most of the school is here. Actually I see more people at this party than I ever see at school.

Nia leans down and hollers in my ear.

"Now, Bobby?"

It's cool, I think, that she still feels like she wants to dance. She looks good dancing, even though she's really far along. She's been dancing with everybody.

Her and K-Boy haven't sat down all night.

Some girl trips over my feet and falls onto the couch beside me, spilling her diet soda all over my shirt. I don't think I've ever come home from a party without food or drink on me somewhere.

But that's okay.

I watch everybody dancing, laughing, talking, and stuffing chips in their faces. I'm feeling like an alien. And it goes way past me feeling like I don't belong here. I feel like I don't even know who all these people are or where they came from, and I've known most of them all my life.

Then Nia grabs my hands and we're dancing in the crowd. Somebody knocks over one of Mrs. Halem's vases and is trying to hide it behind a big-ass plant in the kitchen.

No way would I have even half these people in our apartment, but Jess isn't sweatin' it. She's over in the corner shaking her head at something "Moss" Green and J. L. are saying. Then she shrugs and goes off to dance with one of her friends who looks like she's had too much party.

She waves to Nia and screams over the music, "Haven't been this many people in the place since my Bat Mitzvah. Less fights, too."

Nia starts giggling and yells back, "Definitely less fights."

Then to me, "Two of her uncles seriously threw down in the kitchen. Her aunt ended up throwing a punch bowl, and her mom got so upset she threw up on the caterer."

"Good time, huh?"

"Oh yeah, too bad you missed it."

Then Nia smiles and I remember why I think of her all the time.

We slow dance even though the music is techno, rap, then techno again. She looks tired now, and dancing any faster would probably knock her out.

I take her hand and pull her toward the door. The smoke's starting to get to me. We walk down the hall toward the stairs. One of Jess's neighbors gets off the elevator, pulls a grocery cart behind him, stops and listens to the party. He shoots me and Nia a nasty look, and then goes into his apartment.

It echoes when I close the door, and we sit on the tiled green stairs. Nia leans against me, and for a minute I think she's asleep. She starts to breathe in and out in time with me. She's been so quiet she scares me when she says, "So what are we gonna do, Bobby?"

"About what?"

She puts my hand on her stomach and the

baby kicks. Her question probably scared it, too.

I can't answer, 'cause I really don't know what we're going to do. I'm thinking about what's going to happen, but I don't know what to feel.

I can't imagine a real baby.

Can't imagine going over to Nia's parent's house and holding the baby while they look at me and make me sweat and my stomach hurt. As it is, I make sure they aren't home when I see Nia now.

Can't imagine changing diapers or even feeding a baby 'cause I never had before. I'm the youngest in my family. People fed and put diapers on me.

I say, "We'll be okay. Our parents are gonna help."

"Yeah, I know—but in the end it's all up to us."

"I guess it's always been up to us."

She leans against me again. "I don't want to do it."

"Do what, Nia?"

"I don't want to be anybody's mother. I'm not done with being a kid myself. I'm way too young and so are you."

"No choice now."

She gets up and walks toward the door.

"My mom talked about adoption, but I don't

know if that would make me bug. I mean the idea that I could be passing my own kid every day and not know it. And what about college? A baby, then?"

I get up and wrap my arms around her 'cause we'd made the decision by waiting so long. We didn't want to face it, but now it's all in our face. Nothing to do but get on with it 'cause it's happening no matter how freaked out we get.

Nia tells everybody that they have to take her like she is.

I always have.

I still do.

Nia opens the door, but backs up when cigarette smoke hits her in the face. The party's getting louder.

She walks back over to me. "Wanna dance, Bobby?"

I do.

part IV

now

My brother Paul holds Feather, and she smiles drooly baby gums at him while her arms jerk up and down. He's good with her.

He's good with everybody.

His two kids, Nick and Nora (he got their names from his favorite movie characters), crawl all over the floor and Mary. Fred is in the kitchen making fajitas, and if I close my eyes I can remember that this was the way it used to be.

Paul remembers too, 'cause he looks over at me and smiles. I like having him here. All of a sudden I don't feel so alone.

"Cute kid," he says, then changes holding arms. Feather keeps making happy baby noises. And when Nick and Nora run over to their dad, they start to kiss her all over her face and head. Most times she'd scream. Now she gurgles and jumps.

"Yeah, she's pretty cute."

"Does she give you much trouble?"

I pull at Feather's feet, bare for once, even though mom keeps eyeing her socks on the couch, from across the room.

"Normal stuff. Too much baby sh—err crap, sleepless nights, seriously cranky me. . . ."

Paul watches Nick and Nora sing a song to Feather.

"That's it in the beginning. It ain't pretty."

"You tellin' me?"

"Yeah, well I guess you know, Bobby. It gets better, though. I mean the crawling and first steps make you so happy. Then it freaks you 'cause you know they're slowly getting away from you and heading for the world."

All I can do is shrug to that, 'cause the thought had crossed my mind at two in the morning once how I was going to be a lot happier helping this kid with homework than I was changing a bad case of formula diarrhea.

Nora crawls in my lap and smiles up at me. She looks like Paul. Tall, skinny, black eyes, and always smiling. I can't tell who Nick looks like 'cause he hasn't sat still since he got here.

Mom says it's too much sugar.

Paul says it was him sitting too long in the car.

I say the boy hasn't ever sat still in his whole life, so why are they making excuses for it now?

I like Nick, though, 'cause he's harder to deal with. Nora is easy to like, but I love them both.

Nick is the six-year-old from hell. The good kind of hell, where they play music all day long and get on the nerves of everybody that was ever born, but it's still a good time.

"What's up, Nick?"

He smiles, pinches Nora—she ignores him—and tells me he helped his dad fix the sink a couple days ago.

"How'd that go for you?"

"It was okay till Daddy told me too late not to pour the orange juice down the sink."

Paul's frowning.

"I had the pipes out. Orange juice burns when it gets in your eyes, and besides, I almost drowned."

Dad starts laughing from the kitchen. Mary thinks it's pretty funny too, and I figure they're really laughing so hard 'cause they know Nick won't be living with either of them, so everything he does makes them happy.

Paul looks at them, shakes his head, and says, "It's the revenge theory. They're laughing at me for everything I ever did to them when I was a kid."

"I'm toast then." I look over at Feather who looks like she'll laugh any minute. I know I'm toast. It's been a hell of a year so far for Mary and Fred thanks to me.

Paul laughs, "Feeling doomed?"

"Oh yeah."

"It's a good doomed. Even though I still think you're too young."

"I hear that."

Paul looks sorry for me. He's the only one that didn't say the obvious when he found out I'd gotten Nia pregnant. I felt better telling him than anybody. He was the one person who I knew would say what I needed to hear. I don't remember the exact words, but I felt good when he said them.

"Want to go for a walk, Bobby?"

I nod and take Feather from him to start getting her ready, but Mary comes over and takes her from me.

"Your dad and I will keep all the kids. You two go off and hang out for the rest of the afternoon."

I must look like I'm in shock 'cause Mom

never has said or done that for me since Feather's been here. But now she's looking at me like I'm a baby that just walked across the room for the first time.

Maybe I just did.

I'm laughing so hard at my brother telling me about his neighbors in the little town in Ohio he lives in. He lives near Lake Erie in a place called Heaven. He moved there to be close to his kids after he divorced his wife, Melanie.

He says, "I never thought I could live in a small town."

We get pretzels on the corner and walk toward the movie theater.

"I always dreamed of living in a small town. Green grass, creeks, cows. That all seems perfect. Especially because me and Feather are going back to Brooklyn to live with Dad. I guess it's his turn now. Anyway, I miss the old neighborhood."

"What happened? Why are you going back to Brooklyn?"

"There was a thing. I blew off school and things got stupid. Postal baby-sitter, cops, etcetera, etcetera. Mary's out of town too much and Fred thinks I need more prison guard time.

You know, the kid with the baby needs to be treated like one."

We sit down on the benches in the rec center playground, finish our pretzels, and watch the kids.

Just sittin' quiet.

Finally Paul says, "What about college for next year? What's the good of you being able to graduate when you're sixteen if you're not going to college?"

"I figure I'd just get a Mcjob for a year and try to save some money."

"You'd get to spend more time with Feather."

I look at Paul and then at the running, screaming kids jumping up and down on the playground. Feather will be them one day, and I'll be one of the scared, happy, mad, yelling, smiling parents who sit on the benches and watch. Just watch it all happen.

I say it like I've known it forever, only now it's so clear and I can say it: "I've never been closer to or loved anybody more than I love Feather."

Paul throws a ball back to a group of kids over by the slide and says, "I know that, kid. I know that."

then

The office has babies, kids, and smiling adults hugging and happy all over the walls. I'm holding Nia's hand. Her back's been aching all day, and even me trying to bribe her with pizza, no anchovies, only makes her moan.

Her mom and my dad are sitting behind us. I don't want to turn around and see Fred's face. The last time I looked at him in the cab, he looked a little wigged.

Mrs. Wilkins sometimes leans forward and rubs Nia on the shoulders. I'm thinking it's not really making Nia feel any better. Every time her mom touches her she jumps like she's being hit.

But it's just a reflex.

• • •

If we give our baby up, we could get on with it. Go to college. Go on spring break. Go to parties. Come home on breaks with dirty laundry like my brothers did, and eat everything in the cabinets and fridge.

We could hate our roommates, their music, and their friends. Lie to our parents about our midterm grades and how when they called late on a Tuesday we were at the library.

I want to stay up all night and meet so many people I forget their names. And I want to meet people I might get to know forever.

I don't want to be here.

I don't want to be at home.

I know I should be listening to everything the social worker (fifth one we've talked to—I forget her name) is saying, but I'm not. I figure if I block it all out I won't have to think about it.

She's talking about parental rights.

Waiting periods.

Counseling during the waiting period.

Open adoption.

And all I want to do is paint on the walls. Paint me running through the city and over the bridge.

I want to spray black, greens, and reds all over this office and cover the smiling faces of the kids and the grown-ups.

What the hell are they smiling for?

Do they know some secret nobody's told me or Nia? 'Cause we didn't want a baby anyway, and I can't believe we'll be smiling in some damned picture after we do the right thing.

It's the right thing. Everybody says so, and I want to believe the shit everybody says. I want to believe it's unselfish. I want to believe none of this is supposed to be about me.

Then the social worker says, "Now, do you have any questions?"

Nia asks, "Can we meet them? The people who are going to get the baby. . . ."

"Well that goes back to whether you are going to have a traditional adoption or an open one.

"Now . . ." Then she goes on.

This woman is nice and looks us in the face to see if we're getting any of it. Mostly we're not, but she keeps on going.

Nia's tired and sore.

I'm freakin' and in shock when everybody says I should be relieved and throwing a party. The hard part is that they're right and I should be happy. Right?

In a few minutes we're all standing out in the hall. Nia and me lean against the wall and look

Angela Johnson

straight ahead at a billboard that talks about reproductive responsibility.

There's a girl, about thirteen, holding a baby.

We keep leaning against the wall and don't talk to our parents who are shaking the social worker's hand and telling her that they have to make calls and whatever.

I take out some bubble gum and hand Nia a piece.

We're still blowing bubbles when we walk out of the office hand in hand, then get into separate taxis with our parents and head to different parts of the city.

now

I THINK SHE KNOWS we're someplace else.

She just fell asleep on my stomach after being wide-eyed and whining all night long. I feel sorry for her. But it's good to be back in the old hood.

Dad's been poking his head in the room all night, asking if everything is okay and did I need him to take her. The first time he asked I wanted to say, "Take her where?"

But I just shake my head. He leaves my door open like he wants to hear her if she cries.

Mom always shut hers tight. She says so she wouldn't be tempted to do what most grand-mothers would do. Take over.

There still are a whole bunch of times I want

her to take over, even more than I feel right about having. But she never does.

She only ever changed, fed, or rocked Feather to sleep when I didn't need her help. But she warned me. She said I was the parent. She was only the grandparent.

"It's your world, kid," she said a couple days after Feather was born.

After the last of our things were moved into Dad's apartment, she got back into her Jeep and sat there without turning the ignition. I stood on the stoop with Feather, wondering what was wrong.

Hell, she was always in a hurry to be anyplace but where she was. So I walked over to the Jeep and knocked on the window on the passenger side.

She was crying.

Damn, that scared me. I held on to Feather real hard then, and only loosened up when she squeaked.

"Haven't ever seen you cry before, Mom."

Even though she had dark glasses and a hat on, I knew it.

"Check me out, kid, 'cause you won't be seeing me do it again anytime soon. That crying shit is what your old man does."

"Yeah," I say. "He's pretty good at it."

"Yep, that's him, cooking and crying. He always was too sensitive."

She's smiling though.

"And that's why I know you two are going to be fine with him. He'll baby both of you."

"Not like you, huh?"

She leans back, then starts the car up.

"No, not like me, and that's a good thing. I don't think you and your brothers could have stood *two* parents like me."

I stand back and she rolls the window up, then blows two kisses and heads back home.

When I turn around, Dad is standing on the stoop with a baby quilt. "Isn't it getting too chilly out here for the baby?"

And a cup of coffee for me.

We walk back to the apartment and I fall asleep with Feather asleep on me surrounded by our boxes.

I wake up to different neighborhood sounds, but it all comes back. It's five thirty in the morning and I'm walking Feather around, looking out the windows of the apartment.

I put on coffee for Dad and open boxes that I don't want to think about unpacking. No hurry,

Fred says. He knows how busy I am with the last of school and the baby.

Whenever will be okay.

I kiss the top of Feather's curly head and hold her close. She shivers a little, so I grab my Mets sweatshirt and wrap her in it.

She yawns and looks at me like she's going to ask me something, and I'll be damned if she doesn't look just like Nia.

She looks at me with those eyes that know me.

I know then that even when everything's changing, Feather's not gonna mind as long as she's with me.

then

NIA SAYS SHE'S BEEN HAVING DREAMS that she's in a nest. When my mom says from her darkroom—which used to be a walk-in closet—"That makes sense. You know, babies and nesting," Nia leans back on the pillows she's propped up behind her on the floor and says, "No, it's not like that. It was a bad dream 'cause I wasn't a bird. I was this small person in a nasty bird's nest with all kinds of old pieces of clothes and bones. . . ."

"Jeez," J. L. says, then sucks down the gallon of soda he always has with him.

K-Boy stares at Nia. "So what did you do when the bird tried to feed you some already chewed-on worms?"

Nia rolls her eyes at him. "You always know exactly what to say that's going to make me barf."

K-Boy puts his feet on the back of Nia's pillow until she twists around and knocks them off. "Could you be more annoying, or are you waiting for somebody to knock you down before you do it again?"

"Waiting."

"Yeah, okay." Nia starts to rub her lower back. It's eight months now. She must be tired of being pregnant. Anyway, in a month it'll all be over. We decided the other day, it would all be over.

Nia cried.

I cried.

My dad cried.

But we were the only ones. My mom and Nia's parents looked like they just got released from Oz, and not the one with the yellow brick road. I think Nia's dad took his first real breath since the first time he found out she was having a baby.

Her mom smiled at me—which freaked me out.

The baby was going to one of those happy, smiling people in the pictures. It would live in a house with a yard and a dog and a swing set. All the pictures had yards and dogs.

It would all be back the way it was before, in a month. Nothing would have changed. We'd leave school and keep on going.

No baby in a month.

Angela Johnson

now

FEATHER CRIED YESTERDAY when I left her at the sitter's. It's the first time she ever cried for me. I didn't know it till Jackie told me today, though.

"Look at the way she frowns up when you walk away. She did it when you left her yesterday, too."

"Really?"

"Oh yeah. What? Does that surprise you?" Jackie picks up a little girl who just started walking and was hanging on to her pants.

Feather's in her carrier, kicking and smiling now that I'm in her face. I lean close to her and smell her sweet baby head and kiss her cheeks.

Now it's hard to go. Now that she knows

when I'm not around it's so hard to go. And now I look at her and I see Nia. All the way through her I see Nia.

K-Boy waits across the street at the Laundromat. J. L. is spinning around in one of the dryers.

"Hey, man, what took you so long? J. L. got in the dryer when he thought he saw the principal crossing the street for a smoke."

I walk over to the dryer and stop it.

J. L. starts laughing while he's still inside. He's all tangled up in somebody's comforter.

"Crazy much, J. L.?"

He falls out of the dryer and folds the comforter and puts it on the big wooden table over by the vending machines.

"Naw, man. Just cold and tired of not falling down when I walk a straight line. What took you so long?"

"Uh, there's this thing called school. Leaving it before two thirty can get you busted to detention or worse; having to tell your dad he has to leave work to talk to the guidance counselor, again."

K-Boy eats popcorn and reads a fashion magazine, leaning against a washer.

"We gonna do this or what?" he says.

Angela Johnson

J. L. keeps looking at the dryer like he wants to get back in it.

K-Boy says, "Is this going to be a thing with you, man? I mean, you gonna be calling up your friends outside of laundries asking for change and spin time?"

J. L. grabs the magazine from K-Boy, and we all go out the back way through the alley. It's been our (and everybody else's that goes to our high school) getaway since, ever.

We head off through the city, feeling the way you feel when you just got out of something like the dentist or a test. We talk and eat junk all the way to Grand Central.

An hour later we're on a train headed out of the city. Heading out of the city to see Nia.

Feather has sweet sticky marks on her face where the baby who just learned to walk's been trying to share ice cream with her. Every time the little girl comes near her she kicks and shows her gums in a smile that's begging for more of what's on her face.

I scoop up the diaper bag, Mr. Moose, her favorite thing to gum on, and Feather and head out the door with Jackie reminding me Feather has a doctor appointment tomorrow. We walk out into the sun with kids running up and down the sidewalks.

Everybody's out.

It's April and summer doesn't feel like something so far away anymore. Feather sighs and blinks when a beam of sun hits her in the face.

Now we're only three blocks from Jackie's house. No subway to get her there. No getting up three hours before school starts.

Some kids my age are hanging around this arcade I've been wanting to check out, but haven't had the time, and probably won't ever have. They lean against the games and each other. I look at them and feel like I'm missing something.

Then I think—I got K-Boy and J. L. I mean not like before. But I still got them. It'll never be like before, but I still got 'em.

I get to our building and go up the elevator.

"We're home, baby."

She knows it 'cause all of a sudden she seriously needs a diaper change.

Dad's left a note on the fridge that I see when I go to make Feather a bottle:

FOOD IN THE FRIDGE. A LETTER FROM
YOUR BROTHER.

I feed Feather and read my letter from Paul out loud. She relaxes in my arms, and after a few minutes the formula in her bottle isn't as important as sleeping is. I take her to our room and try to put her in her crib, but she isn't that sleepy.

She just looks pissed and dares me to put her down.

So I don't, and keep reading to her. When I'm done reading I sit holding her by the bedroom window and tell her what I did today. And just about the time her eyes close shut, I tell her about her mom.

then

I USED TO WATCH COMMERCIALS when I was little. I'd run in from the bedroom I shared with my brother Nick every time one came on.

I knew all the words to commercials for floor cleaner and cars, breakfast cereals and soda, fast food places and car batteries. I knew 'em all and used to sing commercials day in and out.

I'm singing a video rental commercial to Nia's stomach now. Since the baby won't be talking to me as it's growing up this has to be enough, even if it is just stupid commercial jingles.

Nia thinks it's cute, and looks at me like I'm a puppy, then curls up on the couch and goes to sleep. I sing a few more commercials to the baby, then get up to leave.

I'm still dodging her parents. I can't help it. K-Boy laughs at me about it, but he spends his time trying to feel superior. I got reason.

I touch Nia on the back before I head out the door, leaving her smiling in her sleep. I walk onto the street singing a shampoo commercial.

Nia

WHEN I WAS FIVE I wanted to be a firefighter. All my uniforms would have Nia on them, and I would speed through the city in the lightning trucks. I wanted the ladders to rise high into the sky and have me on them. I wanted my hands to pull people from fires and disasters. I wanted my arms to be the arms that carried out babies and kids, safe. I wanted my feet to be the ones that ran up endless flights of stairs and brought everybody back alive.

But by the time I was ten I wanted to be a balloonist, and just fly up high over everybody, and that's what it feels like I'm doing now.

I'm flying up high over everybody; way over the city and even myself. I'm flying over Bobby and my parents, *and the park with all my friends in it. I guess this is what it must feel like to be dying.*

All I want to do is lie here and sleep, even though I see the blood and it shouldn't be where it is. And it was just a minute ago Bobby was singing a shampoo commercial, but he's gone now.

But that's okay because all I want to do is fly.

now

I tell Feather about her mom.

She never liked to wear shoes, but always had to, 'cause you do when you're surrounded by cement. She liked tacos better than anything, and always ate the extra sauce straight out of the packet.

She cheated at cards and didn't care who knew. Socks got on her nerves, and she had fifty pairs of sunglasses and seventy hats.

She got in fights at school when she saw somebody being mean to somebody else, even though she could be mean too and very funny.

While she was pregnant with you, fish made her sick, but she ate spicy food all the time.

And all she wanted to do while she was pregnant was swim, but she'd never learned how.

There's a picture of her right before you were born, with a big smiling face painted on her stomach. She liked to sit on the floor and hide under tables so she could eavesdrop.

You look just like her in baby pictures.

Feather stretches, yawns, then opens her eyes for a second before she snores once and goes back to sleep.

I tell her, I saw your mom today.

K-Boy told her jokes that she probably didn't hear, and J. L. played her his new CD and danced around her bed till one of the nurses came in and gave him a nasty look.

I told her what I was going to wear to graduation, and how you preferred the night to the day, liked ice cream already, and how Mr. Moose made you smile.

I asked her if she remembered how I put you on her stomach before they took her away from the city and away to the country for something called long-term care. I asked her if she was ever going to wake up, and if she really believed what the doctors said to her parents about brain damage.

I told her about you and how you were mine, not the smiling, happy people's baby; 'cause now that she was gone I wouldn't sign the papers.

I got tired after a while and J. L. went looking for food, then K-Boy went to sleep on the chair beside her bed, but I kept telling her about you, Feather.

The nurse came in and turned her over.

Another nurse came in and cleared her breathing tube.

But it didn't matter what was going on, baby; I kept telling her about you.

Damn right, I kept telling her about you.

Angela Johnson

then

I TRIED NOT TO RUN, but I did.

I tried not to cry, but when I looked down at my shirt it was soaked; with me wanting to believe it was sweat. By then, though my nose was running and I couldn't even see the faces of the people, I ran into the street.

And I must have been screaming. . . .

Must have looked crazy and desperate, but it was better for me to run all the way to the hospital from my mom's 'cause the note on the door said meet her there, something had happened to Nia.

The whacked part was I didn't start trying to make a deal with God till I was almost running through the doors. And when I see my mom's face I know I got to catch up.

So I start begging.

I say how it's supposed to work out 'cause we thought about it. We made a mistake but we aren't stupid. We were going to do the right thing.

Then I guess I start babbling about how Nia looks when she sleeps and how she smiles and eats and laughs, but I have to stop 'cause even though I don't think about God or go to church, maybe this isn't the way you make deals with him.

Maybe he doesn't listen if you scare everybody in the emergency room and hold on to your mom that tight while you're screaming and crying more than you ever have in your whole damned life.

Maybe if you'd said out loud how much you felt in the beginning you wouldn't have to look at her parents' faces when they walk out the automatic double doors.

And my mom's whispering in my ear, past the screaming, "Hold on, Bobby, hold on," like she did when I had poison ivy all over my body when I was nine and she held my hand while I cried on cool white sheets.

Hold on, Bobby. Hold on.

I want to tell Mr. Wilkins to hold on to his wife harder 'cause right in front of the doctors, nurses,

Angela Johnson

me, and my parents she's starting to disappear.

In a minute, it's too late.

She's gone.

Just like that. No noise. Not a word.

She walks over to the window and looks out it like she's a tourist. She's seeing everything for the first time and she doesn't even know us.

She's holding Nia's favorite stuffed animal, and all I can think is she grabbed it to make Nia feel better, but when I look at her again, I change my mind.

It's for her.

We all sit at a round table, but none of us are knights.

My parents make soft sounds at Nia's parents and ask the doctor questions.

Nia's father nods his head at everybody and cries when the doctor closes his folder, pats him on the back, and leaves. Mrs. Wilkins holds hands with her husband, but I don't know how she keeps a grip, 'cause she's been invisible since the emergency room.

I can't ever be a knight or brave, so I ask nothing about brain death or eclampsia or why the girl who had a thousand pair of sunglasses and my baby inside her won't ever walk, talk, or smile again. And I have to say irreversible vegetative coma five times, like a tongue twister, to believe it.

And I feel like a three-year-old when I walk out the room between my parents while they hold my hands. Mr. Wilkins starts crying, then falls to his knees, and it's only then that Nia's mom comes back from the invisible place and rocks him in her arms.

I carry around a picture of me, Nia, K-Boy, and J. L. at the beach. A minute before the picture was taken by J. L.'s sister we were all out in the water, splashing around, having fun.

I had to fold the picture in half so it would fit in my wallet. I like the way Nia's laughing and the rest of us look pissed.

Nia's laughing 'cause just as the picture is snapped she tells us she's given all our clothes to some kids who said they needed them for Halloween.

It was July, but we believed her.

J. L.'s sister has the next picture of us running back to the water. It doesn't show our faces, only our backs while we chase her out into the white water.

I guess I think of it when I turn around in the waiting room and see the backs of both my buddies talking to my dad. But I know they won't be

Angela Johnson

laughing like we did, or yelling "Get her" like we did.

But they're here, and she won't ever be running away from any of us again. In a few minutes, though, they're beside me and in the white light of the waiting room. I miss Nia for the first time, but feel her more than I ever did.

It wasn't fast or blurred. Didn't knock me out or make me fall against the wall.

She came to me slowly.

Somebody covered in hospital clothes head to foot pushed the incubator toward me down the longest hall I've ever been in.

My mom and dad talked over my shoulders, and Mr. and Mrs. Wilkins cried over by the nurses' station.

She came to me so slowly I felt like I was in a dream. Four steps away, three, then two . . .

Then she was all dark hair, hands in fists, Nia's nose and mouth. She came to me so slow, and it was just like somebody brushed the air with a feather.

I just came from the nursery.

Feather doesn't like being wrapped up in her blanket. She fights against the binding. I like that she does that. I like that the only thing that makes her not fight is me holding her in the rocking chair in the hospital family room.

It's been an hour since I did it.

The social worker tried about five minutes of reasoning. She kept tapping her pencil against her desk. I think she was saying the things she thought she should say.

"I know this is an emotional time for you, Bobby. I can't think what you must be going through. Nia's condition—have the doctors said anything else?"

I look at the smiling families on the wall.

"They keep saying 'persistent vegetative.' I hate when they say it, but there it is."

"Bobby, the baby . . ."

"Feather. Her name is Feather."

"We have to think in the end what's best for her. Are you ready for this? Do you know what raising a baby entails?"

I look at the adoption papers stacked in front of me, then fold them in half before I tear them.

"No, I don't know anything about raising a kid. I'm sixteen and none of those people on the wall look like the kind of family me and Feather's gonna be. But I'm doing it."

The social worker's forehead wrinkles up.

Angela Johnson

"You don't have to do it. This baby is wanted. There's a family that wants her. They're set up to take her and love her—"

"But *I* love her, and even though I'm not set up for her, she's mine. And I'm hers."

When I walk out of the office I think I see "Just Frank" standing at the end of the hall. And then I know I'm being a man, not just some kid who's upset and wants it his way.

I'm being a man.

Before all the papers turned into shreds, I talked to Nia's parents.

I talked; they listened.

They talked; I listened.

They cried.

I almost cried.

And when Mrs. Wilkens started telling me how much the baby looked like Nia and she's all they'll ever have of their daughter, I did start to cry. But I wiped my eyes real fast on the back of my sleeve 'cause I'm going to be this baby's daddy now.

I don't know any of the parent rules, but crying like a baby when you just decided to keep a baby probably shouldn't happen.

"We'll support you keeping the baby, Bobby,"

was all they said in the end. But when they looked at the baby through the nursery glass, it was like they were saying good-bye.

Soon Feather is home with me sleeping on my stomach.

Three days ago everything was different. She wasn't here and she was never going to be with me.

Now she's three days and nine hours old, won't sleep through the night, and my mom— her grandmother—only smiles at her when I'm not looking. But it's all okay 'cause I know now better than I ever did that I'm supposed to do this. I'm supposed to be her daddy and stay up all night if I have to. I'm supposed to suck it up and do all the right things if I can, even if I screw it up and have to do it over.

It's all right for now, 'cause for the first time I get to watch the coming of the soft morning light.

now

BABY, DO YOU WANT TO hear more about Heaven? Do you want to know more about the fields, and grass, and cows? Do you want to wonder what it would be like to have a deer wake you up by eating on a tree outside your window?

Do you want to know more about somewhere else that's not here?

"What you thinking about, Bobby?"

I jump 'cause I think it's the first time my dad has ever asked me this question. And, because it's the first time, I think I should come up with something good.

What to say?

I got a little time to think. Feather went down

for a nap a minute ago and won't wake up till her formula digests and she needs some more. For once I don't have anything to do and the sun is shining down Seventh Ave.

What to say?

Do I say I'm glad I'm back in Brooklyn and wanted more than anything for Feather to see more trees? Do I tell him I'm glad I'm back with him 'cause he puts the covers over me at night and kisses Feather all the time before he leaves the room?

Or do I tell him that I'm thinking I need something else 'cause of everything that's happened? Everything.

Do I tell him how my whole body hurt when I went to see Nia in the nursing home the other day? Do I describe how skinny she is and how soft her lips were when I kissed her good-bye?

Maybe I'll just tell him how I don't think I'll make it if I stay here. In this place. In this state.

Maybe I'll just tell him how I feel like I'm a baby with a baby most of the time. Just playing daddy until somebody comes over and says, "Hell, kid, time's up. No more of this daddy thing for you, and anyway you've been busted."

Maybe I'll tell him how all of a sudden the city just feels like it's too big and I've been having

Angela Johnson

dreams that I leave Feather on the subway and can't get back inside the train fast enough to get her, and she disappears forever.

Maybe I should tell him all that and then he'll make me something good to eat and we'll turn on one of the sports channels and watch baseball all into the night.

Instead I say, "Paul says he loves Ohio and it's a good place to raise kids."

Dad goes over to the window and squints into the sun.

"Your brother might be right, Bobby, he just might be right."

And then me and Dad turn on the sports channel and talk about how we should have checked the Mets out more.

heaven

I WON'T TALK about the good-byes.

I won't talk about how for a month I went to every place in the city that I loved so much, so many times that K-Boy and J. L. thought I was whacked.

I won't say how much I'm going to miss everybody and how if it wasn't for Pennsylvania I'd be one hour from Brooklyn instead of eight and I'd have the best of all of it.

I won't say.

I won't talk about how, I woke up one night to my mom rocking Feather and telling her to mind me and take care of me.

I will talk about how, when I finally visited Paul in Heaven, Ohio, the town was out of some old postcard and Feather smiled at everybody when we walked down the main street.

I will talk about how the grass smelled and how the horses looked running in the fields outside of town. And how I decided the little apartment by the car repair shop with its big front window and bikers hanging around all day had to be ours.

I will talk about how I didn't know if it would all work out as me and Feather pulled out of New York on the bus, and waved to everybody we'd left behind.

I can talk about how it felt to be holding my baby in my arms on the long ride, getting off the bus when we had to and sleeping the rest of the time.

I can tell you how it feels sitting in the window with Feather pointing out the creek that rolls past our backyard. I can tell you how it is to feel as brand new as my daughter even though I don't know what comes next in this place called Heaven.

sweet, hereafter

For those who did and did not come home

Prologue

THERE'S A FRONT PAGE PHOTO OF MY friend Jos standing by the side of a road on a hot summer day. I almost don't recognize him, because he's out of place. It's a frozen moment in time—but I'm so used to Jos being animated, funny and moving. It bothers me that one picture can define everything in other people's minds but never really tell the whole story.

A cop in dark shades is touching him on the arm. Gently. The photographer was close, 'cause you can see every line on the cop's and Jos's face. There weren't any lines an hour before.

. . .

It's early. Everything is quiet. Too quiet. I turn on the radio to make sure there hasn't been some kind of world-ending disaster. Hell—they do happen. More than you could ever dream they do. I've seen them, been a part of them, don't even have to watch the news to see one happening.

My feet are cool on the old hardwood floors, and I don't even mind that I'm still trying to work out a splinter. I walk to the front window.

I love the cool.

And I love the feeling I get knowing I'm walking on floors people walked on a hundred years ago. I blow the candle out 'cause finally the sun is struggling past the clouds.

The radio crackles as I stare out at Lake Erie haze.

I press my face against the window and feel cobwebs on the side of my head but don't pull back. If I listen close I can hear cars blowing past on the road about a hundred yards away.

I listen for Curtis over the drone of the radio—I do it without thinking. Then I see the groundhogs through the window and start peeling apples for them.

I do it like I breathe or walk to the sink to get a glass of water.

Angela Johnson

Automatic.

It starts to rain, and I watch like the photographer did on that burning hot summer day, while rain streaks every inch of the window.

Curtis

1

THERE ARE LONG ARMS ALL AROUND ME
and I know I'm gonna have a serious curb put
on my social life if I don't get off this couch
right now and go home.

When I try to get up, Curtis's arms squeeze
me more, and I know that I'm not going
anywhere, not until he gives it up and lets go.

Still, I'm thinking I got so much homework
I'll be up all night trying to finish it. And if I
want the parents outta my business I have to
keep the low B going. I ain't never been an A
student, so my parents are happy about those Bs
I drag out every semester.

And there's Curtis. . . .

I'd miss him if I were grounded for life. I'd

miss the way he always smells like sweet leaves underfoot in the fall. I mean, that's what I think of when I'm close to him. The woods. Leaves. Pine needles.

And the feel of his skin . . .

Shit like that. . . .

I don't say shit like that when I'm with Curtis, 'cause he doesn't swear. And even though he's never said anything when I do—I do my best not to do it in front of him.

Raised by a religious grandma is all he'll say about it.

I'm cold.

I'm cold and awake, and he's not here. No arms pull me back. I walk to the open window and smell the woods. I miss Curtis in his place on the couch beside me.

But I live here now too. So when I lean out the window to see what kind of morning sky is out there, I see Curtis, leaning against a tree. And just like that—the cold is gone.

Angela Johnson

2

THE DAY I LEFT HOME, MOST OF MY JEANS were in the washer, and once I was gone, I wondered what I would have to wear. If you slam the hell out of your front door, you better have your bags packed and everything you're going to need with you.

It don't look good to have to come back an hour later to get your shit.

I left home on a sunny day.

I left home on pot roast day.

I left home the day my brother scored three goals at his soccer match.

I left home the day our neighbor's cat got stuck up a tree.

I left home the day I couldn't find my house keys.

I left home the day the mailman delivered about a thousand catalogues.

I left home the day I accidentally broke my favorite CD.

I left home the day I couldn't think of a good reason to stay. I left home, and two days later nobody came for me, so I stayed where I was.

Which is here, in the woods in an old cabin surrounded by trees, bushes, and things that look harmless in the daytime but scratch the door in the night.

I left home, and Curtis told me to come right on in and stay until I was happy not to stay.

The day I left home, I had to go back for my jeans, but I didn't have to go in. They were waiting for me folded in a box outside the front door.

Curtis doesn't talk much. Some days he hardly speaks at all. In the end he tells me what he needs to tell me by smiles, touches, or the tilt of his head. I don't mind. I love the quiet. I love his quiet.

I like living here in the cabin with him, and I know he wants me here. I walk through the cabin and touch the books that are lined against the wall. And there's just enough to remind me of him every day—just enough. Just enough to make you comfortable, but not enough to tell you too much about Curtis. And I didn't know that when I walked in the door, but that's the way it stayed.

I just know him—enough.

And that's okay, 'cause most people only know me enough. My own family only knew parts of me. My friend Marley knew a few parts. I've had secret parts of me since I was little. I'm used to it, and I guess it makes sense I'd love the secret parts of another.

3

THE BOARD SAYS IN PINK CHALK—

THE REVOLUTION WILL
NOT BE TELEVISED—SO
READ A FUCKING BOOK.

Ms. Jameson is way mad.

And everybody thinks they know who did it. So we all sit around with stupid looks on our faces glancing toward the back of the room at Carl.

AGB. Angry Goth Boy.

Black nail polish—kicked out for two weeks for turning over desks and screaming "fascist" at the art teacher when she was talking about the Impressionists.

Now I remember why I decided to take up merchandising and not be held hostage in rooms with thirty other people five days a week.

Ms. Jameson puts the evil eye on Carl.

He smirks at her.

I like Carl, though. We used to skip class together, back in middle school.

"So who will start today?" she says.

I don't remember too much after that until somebody taps me on my back and I jump.

Brodie.

"Was I snoring?"

Brodie starts to laugh. Even though I haven't turned around, I'd know that laugh anywhere. He can't ever hold it in, and I can't count how many times we've gotten busted because of that laugh.

"Brodie!"

"Sorry, Ms. Jameson."

And I go back to sleep and start to dream again. This time I know I'm dreaming. I'm sitting on the side of the road and it's raining. I've always loved being in the rain. Now a man that I realize I should know but can't remember his name walks up to me. It could be Jos or even my brother. In my dream the familiarity is just there. I can't tell if his face is wet because of the rain or because of the tears. And even in my dream all I want to do while I'm sitting there is to go after the photographer and beat the hell out of her for freezing this man's crying face in my mind. But it's just a dream.

I walk out of school with Brodie and try to remember how we came to be friends. He's a jock, class president, and dates cheerleaders—but he's funny, kinda twisted, and mad smart. And I'm pretty sure the class president thing was just so he could get snack machines in the senior lounge.

"I need a ride," he says.

"Alice is funny about who she gives rides to. Last time you were in her, there was that thing . . ."

"Dag, Sweet. All I did was change the radio a few times and mess with the heat. That shouldn't make a truck stall."

Brodie busts open a bag of chips and laughs while throwing some at three sophomore girls walking by. They laugh and scream his name.

"Cute." I pull Alice out of the parking lot.

"I know," he says.

"Where do you need to go, then?"

"I don't know—just drive. Or we could go get food. There's only so many chips I can eat before I start to starve to death."

Angela Johnson

I slow down for a dog crossing the road.

"Snack machines not working out so hot, huh?"

Brodie turns and looks at me like I just went through his underwear drawer. Then he looks hurt. I laugh. Then I remember it's the reason I introduced Brodie to my friend Jos: Sometimes they're both just too much fun and full of shit. They play well together and make me laugh.

"C'mon, Brodie—class president? You'd rather be watching football or some crazy cartoon with people as underwater creatures or dogs and cats playing saxophones . . ."

"Yeah, okay, that's me."

"Yeah, but why don't most people know that about you?"

"You do. But that's who you are," he says.

"What do you mean, that's who I am?"

Brodie finishes up the chips and sticks the empty in his courier bag.

"Yo, Sweet, have you ever really looked at yourself in a mirror?"

"Where you going with this—way to get the subject off of you, huh?"

Brodie smiles. "If you ever even acted like you would look at somebody from this school, there'd be a riot. Man, everybody would be creeping around your locker—stalking you.

I don't know what the problem is, 'cause at first like any dumbass guy who gets viciously rebuffed by a mommy, I wanted to believe you just liked girls."

"I do like girls—"

Brodie smacks me with a balled-up bandana he finds on the seat next to him. "You know what I mean. Anyway, whatshisname is lucky."

"His name is Curtis."

Brodie laughs, then hangs out the window and hollers something to a passing car. I pull off the road into the parking lot of Tony's Café.

Me and Brodie jump out the car and head inside. I think about locking Alice but decide not to. Brodie is about four steps ahead of me when he shifts the bag on his shoulder and a box of pink chalk falls out.

Angela Johnson

4

THERE'S A BIG SUGAR MAPLE TREE THAT sits in the corner of the yard. I sometimes lean against it and fall asleep. Curtis always asks me why I'm leaning against myself.

In this cabin with Curtis I wake up to the sound of the wind. Or an animal running underneath the house. Groundhogs have moved in. Well, they've probably always been there.

Curtis likes them.

He calls them the wild pigs and leaves them vegetable scraps and tells me that they like salsa music. He says that he plays salsa music to the groundhogs. Then they come and hang out in the front yard.

I thought he was making it up.

So one day I'm leaning against the tree and there's salsa music coming from the window—and there they were. Three groundhogs sitting and chewing. I sat and watched them for a long time, until it started getting cold. But just when I thought about going back in, Curtis came out the door dressed in camouflage and carrying an old canvas jacket.

He knelt down and wrapped me up in it.

Then he sat down and wrapped his arms around me.

Reason six hundred and ninety-two why nothing should shock me but it always does.

Where we live there is nothing strange about men in full camouflage. You see that stuff in the woods, in the supermarkets, and going down the back roads with gun racks and pickups. I never did understand it. Got used to it, but never understood it. But I still wanted to know why he was covered in the gear.

He could read me.

"I'm in the reserves. Already been to Iraq—probably have to go back."

Curtis took out apple pieces and threw them to the groundhogs.

"You mean the army? I mean, I can get with them when they're rescuing people and shit."

"We do that."

"Did you ever shoot your gun?"

"Weapon," he said.

Curtis threw more apples to the hogs—who now were seriously eating.

"But you're going to college. Why are you in the reserves?"

Curtis frowned and kept pitching apples.

"It's helping me pay. I got this cabin and my car. That's it. I can't sell the cabin. It came from family. It's mine, but I could never sell it. So it's the reserves."

"I thought you were nonviolent, a pacifist. You look sick every time you read about someone getting shot."

Curtis frowned again and said, "They might be coming for me—any day now. Any day."

He leaned against me again and kissed the back of my neck.

"If you've already been, why do you have to go back? I mean, damn it, you got responsibilities. You have to feed the wild pigs. Give them the money back and get a job on campus."

The groundhogs looked up at me like they were thinking, *YOU ARE SUCH A BIG-ASSED LIAR. IT'S ALL ABOUT YOU?*

They were right.

A story Curtis tells.

When he was little, there were always cousins that lived with his family. Sometimes there were as many as thirteen kids in their house. It never mattered. They got by. When his parents were alive, they made a lot of money and believed in sharing everything with everybody.

He was six years old when one of his cousins got sick and had to go to the hospital. She never came back. But because he was only six, the older kids told him she wouldn't be back because a dragon got her. He liked fairy tales, and they thought he would understand.

They didn't let the little kids go to the funeral.

So he stayed home and started going through all his books. Afterward, when the family went to malls, he'd always want to go to the bookstore. He was looking. . . . He was looking in all the fairy tales that had dragons in them. He was looking for his cousin. He expected her to appear in the window of a castle. Or maybe she would be running across a moat. But the girls never looked like his cousin.

They were pale, blond, and looked like teenagers.

Angela Johnson

His cousin was chocolate-skinned, had black plaits, and was five.

He never found her.

The dragon had taken her a long way away and for good.

5

I WATCH THE TELEVISION IN THE FRONT window of Morry's Electronics. The flat screen is so big it takes up the whole window. I blow cigarette smoke over my shoulder. A few minutes ago Jos told me I smelled like a smoke-stack. That's why I try not to get too many fumes on me.

I'm not as into the TV as I'm into what's on it.

There's long lines of troops coming out of a hangar onto a runway. And if you don't look at their faces, you don't see that most of them are so young it's probably the first time a lot of them have ever left their state, let alone the country.

My dad said the fatigues are different than when he was in Vietnam, 'cause they were in a jungle. The colors now are better for the desert.

The farm kids are the same as they were when my dad went to Vietnam. The city kids have that walk . . . like they know where they're going.

I know somebody like that. He walks ahead, sure of himself, and never acts like he doesn't know where he's going. He moves like he was here and did everything before people even walked the planet. He's that comfortable in his skin.

His skin. His skin.

I put my cigarette out and watch as boys and girls, men and women, fill up a whole transport plane, and I feel cold. After a few minutes a woman with a stroller is standing next to me. She watches the TV and moves the stroller back and forth. The baby starts to babble, but in a minute it's asleep.

"I'm so proud," the woman says, her eyes filling up with water. I feel bad for her. I look at her baby and figure her husband or somebody real close to her is going to fight or is already there. I figure she feels sick with worry every day.

"Is someone in your family over there?" I ask.

She keeps moving the stroller and looking at the baby. "Oh, God, no!" she says. "I don't really know anybody in the military. . . ."

She smiles.

I stop watching the TV and look at the baby. And hell, I know this kid already has a college fund. His mom's eyes shine, and I realize she looks like she just stepped out of a spa.

Her skin glows, and she smells like apples in her hooded yellow top and white yoga pants. Her wedge-cut hair catches a breeze. Her diamond tennis bracelet sparkles when she brushes an imaginary hair off her cheek.

And why did she say, "God, no!"? I betcha there's some accountants and doctors over there who had to go into the reserves to pay for their degrees.

She keeps talking.

"I'm proud because we know our safety is at stake, and—well, we really do need to bring these people down. . . ."

I start to light another cigarette but remember the baby and slide the pack back into my jeans.

"What people?"

The woman looks at me the way people look

at children they think are stupid and uncared for—with a mixture of *The schools have failed us* and *I wonder if this child's parents know anything.*

"Those people."

"Who?" I say.

The woman starts to look me over. Black girl, five feet six, curly 'fro, jeans, and T-shirt with dogs on it that says I'M ONLY IN IT FOR THE PUGS.

"Oh, honey . . . You're too young to understand, I guess."

She looks like she wants me to understand. She really does. But she doesn't get how dumb she sounds with those words coming out of her well-made-up lips. I want her to go away. I want her to go back to her well-fucking-appointed house and shut up. I want her to not have an opinion that is not mine. I want her to be somebody else who walked up to this window and talked about how bad and hopeless this all is. I want her to be anybody else but who she is.

I want her to ask me if I know somebody over there.

Then again—no—I don't want her to ask that. She's not special enough to know. I close my eyes and wish her away.

When I open them again, she's still there, so I say—

"All I know is those people never follow me in stores to make sure I'm not stealing, those people don't pull me over for no good reason when I'm driving, and other than that I know about as much about those people as you do about them."

That got rid of her. . . .

In five seconds the woman is moving away from me down the sidewalk and pushing the stroller toward the baby boutique. The kid wakes up, screaming. And I wonder if she would be so damned sure about bombs and guns if her child was running through the desert trying to stay alive.

I pull out my pack from my jeans, light up another cigarette, and finish watching as the talking head smiles her stupid smile and talks about how the army and marines do a great job. I want to grab her through the TV, shake her, tell her to stop reading the script and think for herself.

The army and marines would rock so much better with their asses back here at home.

Angela Johnson

6

How I met Curtis.

Curtis has the darkest eyes. Clear and shining. His eyes are like the girl with the wings, but longing. I met her before I met him. I'd seen his eyes way before I started working in my friend Jos's store. Even though technically that's where I first met him.

I knew his eyes.

Then he smiled at me.

Okay, I thought I knew him as he wandered around the store touching some things and laughing at others. (That Santa with his pants falling down was pretty stupid.) But when he took a pair of silvery wings down from the wall—it was like I'd known him for a long time. And then I knew him. His eyes used to live next door to me.

I used to live on lockdown. It was always for something so minor I couldn't remember what I did a few hours later, but in hindsight know I probably did it. I did what I always did when the parental popo nabbed me. I sneaked out of the house to sit in the backyard, 'cause I was in lockdown—a lot. And I sneaked out—a lot. After a while it was almost like a game. For me, anyway. My parents just gave up thinking they could keep me jailed in my room. And I just did what I did.

I used to watch our next-door neighbor from my lawn chair.

I started noticing the Wing Girl, 'cause she never left the yard. I figure she was probably in her mid-twenties. She had some teenaged brothers and sisters who were older than me, but they all went to JFK, the Catholic high school, and never hung out with anybody in the neighborhood.

She got mailed wings through the UPS. And one day, when she opened them, they fell out from some sparkling green tissue paper shimmering and ready to tie onto her back.

Angela Johnson

And I didn't know then (like I didn't know her name) that there would be a story about her and the wings.

Everybody's got a story.

So I'd sneaked out again to sit in the back-yard, knowing that it was time for the wings.

The only thing that divided our yards were two rose of Sharon trees. And in a few minutes she was out back—big 'fro, bare feet, jeans, and an old T-shirt—unwrapping her wings. She was about ten feet from me, but it didn't look like she knew I was there.

Her new wings were green with yellow and orange butterflies.

She put them on and walked across the yard like she always did. I stood up and watched her. The wing thing was in then—but she was pushing the age limit. Even so, I was drawn to the smile on her face. I thought she might just take off and fly over Heaven.

She walked up and back across the lawn, until after a few minutes one of her brothers came out, took her by the arm, and started to lead her in. She let him. Before he walked away, he turned and stared at me for almost a minute with the darkest eyes I'd ever seen.

. . .

Now here comes the stupid thing. I wanted those wings.

I wanted to sail around my backyard, wings ready to fly me anywhere. I wanted to be the girl over five who could wear wings and have everybody believe it. You know—magical and dreaming of sprites and troll kings. There were a couple of girls I knew who could carry it off. And damn—there was the woman next door.

I wanted not to be of the earth.

I wanted to be winging around in the sky.

A couple of weeks later I took the package from her porch before she could get to it. I saw that the wings came from some shop in New Orleans. The box felt empty.

Stupid, but I wanted them.

I wanted to be as happy as she looked in her wings, but just as I was about to jack the wings, she came out on her porch. She walked out and smiled at me. Just smiled. Then I saw what it was about her. She had an old gash that went from her cheek, up her forehead, on into her hairline. Her eyes were faraway and unfocused.

It wasn't the wings.

I handed her the box.

The rest of the summer was messed up and

Angela Johnson

boring except for the few times when my girl Marley and Bobby busted me out.

But by the end of the summer the Wing Girl and her brothers and sisters were gone. I missed her walking back and forth. Winged and ready to fly.

A couple of years later Curtis walked into the store. When I saw him and looked into his eyes, I saw her eyes—the girl with the wings. He strolled around the store, looking for wings to send to her. His face was kind, and he had his sister's eyes, but they twinkled.

7

CURTIS AND ME STAY UP ALL NIGHT LONG and listen to the water crash against the beach up at Mentor-on-the-Lake. We camp next to the bikers and their families having bonfire cookouts and staying in the cabins all over the woods by Lake Erie.

We usually bring burritos from Taco Tantos and warm 'em up on somebody's fire.

No problem.

Sometimes when it gets real quiet, I think I hear him calling over to someone on the dark beach to turn the music up. He does that. He doesn't care what kind of music it is; he just thinks it should be loud.

And whoever is playing it always turns it up.

I drive up my old street, real slow, and I think I can do it this time. I can turn in to the driveway, turn the truck off, open the door, and get out.

It's okay if I stand by the truck for a few minutes.

It's okay if I think about it for a while too, I don't have to go up to the door like I'm being chased by something. I can take my time.

I can look at the perfect grass.

I can count the petals on the perfect rose bushes.

I can see my reflection in the sparkling front windows.

I can stand and wait before I knock on the door. I won't go running in. I want them to know that I miss them but can do all right without them. I want them to smile when they answer the door and not get that look that says—*What the hell is it?*

I want them to ask me where I've been and if I'm getting enough to eat and am I in a good place. I want them to take me in their damned perfect house and sit me down on the couch and tell me they made pie. Or even bought pie just for me.

I want to be asked to stay to dinner (I always

wanted to have dessert before dinner in that house). And if somebody asked me to play piano—I would. Even if I haven't played for anyone in ten years and used to slam out of the house if anybody said anything about it.

I'd play.

And after all of that if somebody asked me to stay the night, at first I'd say no. I can't. Got something to do and somebody would miss me. I promised a friend. I've got to get up real early the next morning. Or even I don't want to put anybody out.

But maybe my room is now that office my dad always wanted. And maybe I won't get to listen to his story about being so poor when he was little they picked dandelions in the park to eat.

But I would.

I'd listen.

In the end Alice and me roll on by the empty driveway and dark house that used to be my home. I turn the music up, 'cause that's the way it should be, and head back to Curtis and the cabin with a smile on my face.

8

EVEN THOUGH IT'S RAINING AND LOOKS like everything might be flooding, I go for a walk down by the river. It runs about fifty feet behind the cabin. I like to watch the fish. I can sit there for hours.

Most days are so quiet here.

Sometimes here in this cabin I have to turn the volume on the radio-CD player up to the point of me getting a headache to keep it all together. Too much quiet. I don't know anybody who lives in the quiet like me. It would drive my friends crazy. So I don't ask them over.

But that's not the only reason. There are other things.

I got no iPod.

No TV.

No computer.

But there's books lined up and down the walls on bookshelves Curtis built himself from some trees in the woods.

When everybody found out I had left home, it didn't seem to be any big thing. I think they wondered why it took me so long to leave or why my parents took so long to kick my ass out. But when they found out about Curtis—everybody started talking.

You know people always think it's about sex. Everybody is too hooked up on who's doing what to who. And most people were wondering who my who was. Only my friends didn't care that I didn't hook up. But like Brodie said, it makes you dangerous. People can't put you in a box.

I'm not dangerous.

I wore knee-high rain boots and white lipstick for years. Didn't bother me, but I think it pissed people off. I still don't understand. These days it pisses them off that I go to parties and hang but not at school.

I guess most people are like—how the hell did she get here? And who is she? But I always get invited. I always have fun, so even when I'm

Angela Johnson

leaving school for the woods somebody usually yells across the quad—"PARTY TONIGHT, SHOOGY!"

And I drive Alice and probably pick up about five or six people who sit in the back of the truck and ride to some loud-assed party with too much beer in the middle of a field or some rich kid's house whose parents are gone. Me and Brodie usually end up standing around and bitching and complaining about nothing in particular and everything in between.

I sit by the creek after coming out of the woods and only notice that I'm soaked through when I stand up and feel the water run down my legs. I walk, dripping, through the green leaves, stepping over branches, and I watch where I'm going so I don't fall in animal holes or break an ankle on hidden rocks. But I know the way back to the cabin with my eyes closed.

I walk down the path and climb the six steps.

I start stripping everything as soon as I'm inside. I drop my shoes and shirt by the front door, my shorts by the couch, my bra by the bathroom door, and my panties in front of the tub.

I run hot water into the tub as I stare out

the big window above me. With the stone floors and tree brushing against the window, it's like bathing in the woods.

The big claw-foot tub makes up for no iPod, no TV, no people around. I climb in and sink down up to my chin, and that's when I know I've been walking around freezing. The heat feels good. I start to warm up.

There's still enough light to read when I reach for the book I've been keeping on the floor by the tub. It's a story about a girl who takes care of her brother while being haunted by the ghost of a long-dead uncle. And I keep reading till the trees beside the window are hushed but still wet and have blocked out the little bit of sun left.

Angela Johnson

9

A FEW THINGS ABOUT CURTIS . . .

He loves dogs.

He's six feet two.

Never swears.

He hardly eats meat but loves fish.

Loves hip-hop, jazz, baroque, bluegrass . . .

Has seven brothers and sisters.

Has been to Iraq once and doesn't want to go back and doesn't want to talk about it.

His sister Sadie, the Wing Girl, is the oldest child.

He slammed poetry for a few years.

Loves silent movies.

Can recite whole parts of James Baldwin's books.

Was picked up by cops once when he was seventeen 'cause he was in the "wrong" neighborhood.

Isn't bitter, but doesn't trust like he used to.

Is three years older than me.

Didn't say no when I showed up with my box of jeans.

Curtis walks off into the dark of the night, and it's usually after a real bad dream. I hear him cross the floor, pull on clothes and shoes, then disappear out of the room, then out of the little cabin. And for a few days afterward he hardly speaks.

It ain't that he's mad at me—I can tell. He smiles, does what he has to do, and listens to me when I'm talking. But it's like something took his voice away. After a few days his voice comes back. I don't say a word. I don't ask where he goes or ask why he's not talking, 'cause sometimes you almost don't want to know the answer to some things.

I couldn't give an answer to my parents when they asked me why I disappeared for a week last year in my truck.

I couldn't tell them that it was just a long

Angela Johnson

long end to not ever feeling like I was one of them. How do you tell people who love you that? How do you tell them you spent much of your life looking around the rooms of your house and not finding much that might keep you there?

I ain't mad anymore. It doesn't do any good.

But after I left the first time, I knew that was the beginning of the end of my life with my family. I'd spent the days I was gone at the lake or at the Cedar Lee watching art films. I spent a whole two days watching opera on the screen in high def. I love opera now right alongside Jay-Z.

I gave a ride to a woman named Jodie and her little girl Maddie who were broken down on the side of the road. Jodie's cell phone was dead and her little girl (dressed in a tutu and a Cleveland Browns jacket) was late for her recital. I took them to the high school where the recital was taking place. Hundreds of little girls and boys in dance clothes ran, danced, and hopped into the building.

Jodie thanked me for the ride and for letting her use my cell phone (which I'd turned off days before so I didn't have to listen to my parents calling me every few minutes asking me to come home). The recital had been more important than staying with her car until her husband got there. I liked that.

Maddie sang the whole way and was singing when they both got out of the truck and joined the hordes. I thought of my mom. But I still didn't go home.

I spent a few days with Bobby and Feather. Feather would wake me up with toast and shoes in her hands.

We took walks into their backyard and the woods beyond it. Her hand was warm as she held on to mine and pointed out squirrels, birds, and wildflowers. Her curly black hair was wild on her head as she ran past me to find something new under a tree.

Bobby didn't question me as he made the couch up for me to sleep. We just stayed up late talking about nothing. But once, just once, he wanted an answer to something I didn't have an answer to.

"What do you feel connected to, Sweet?"

I sat there surrounded by his canvases and pictures of his family back in New York, Feather's picture books and little-girl toys poking out everywhere. I knew what he was connected to. And he was connected without pain.

Angela Johnson

I couldn't answer the question. I just leaned against him and read him one of Feather's books.

And when I finally went home—I still couldn't tell them why I left. And there was no way I could tell them that even though I was sleeping in my own bed again, I was already gone.

10

IF YOU TELL A SECRET, IT'S OUT IN THE world forever. You can't ever take it back or explain to the person whose secret it was why you gave it up.

If you don't tell a secret, my mom says it's like living in a little bit of hell—forever.

But I don't believe in hell.

At least not the one the pastor in my old church talked about.

I do have secrets.

But maybe it's not a secret at all. Maybe I could always see it in his eyes. Feel it when he was with me one minute and gone the next minute even when I still held him beside me.

So it's best not to tell.

For now.

I asked Jos once what he was doing in a boring little place like Heaven. He smiled.

He said, "I love my strange mother, I guess."

I understood that. Maybe if my own mother was a little stranger and not so upright I wouldn't have wanted to leave her either. But she was a little stiff, well, a whole lotta stiff, and I didn't think I could feel for her what Jos felt for his mom. It was sad, but that was that.

It was so sad me and Jos decided to drive into the city and go to a psychic advisor on the west side near a deserted mill. We'd gotten her number from the *Free Times* beside an ad that said someone needed a part-time gardener and bird sitter.

Her house sat at the end of a pink flamingo and wooly sheep kind of street. All the houses looked like Hansel and Gretel might visit them for something good to eat. We parked behind an SUV with a moon and star painted on the back door. We walked up the steps and were met by a black and white cat that rolled on its back for attention.

I sneezed and smiled. Jos scratched the cat on the tummy and didn't even get clawed.

Then a woman in a white, blue, and peach

jogging outfit came to the door. Jos laughed. Her name was Magda, her hair was blue and purple, and she said she was ninety-six years old. She gave us tea from Botswana in her overcrowded living room. She smelled like roses.

And a few minutes later she was holding Jos's hand so tight he said later he thought she was going to pull it off his arm. She told Jos soon he'd understand more of the world than he wanted to.

She told me that I was destined to come and go.

It was dark and raining when we left her house. The old mill just a ghost shadow in the distance. We realized we'd been there for over three hours talking to Magda—but I swear those are the only two things either of us can remember her saying. We try to remember but can't.

We left the city and drove the hour or so back to Heaven, only talking to each other when a commercial came on the radio. Jos with a sore hand and me with the knowledge that I'd probably never stay still in the world.

11

MARLEY HANGS OUT ALICE'S PASSENGER window and only puts her head in long enough to ask, "You smokin' anymore, girl?"

I feel the pack in the back of my jeans. If I was any kind of girl, I'd have some kind of purse with about fifty thousand things in it, and I could lie.

"Trying."

"I blame your mom."

I say—"You think she intentionally wanted me to catch her nasty habit?"

"I've seen it before. Bonding. Maybe she wanted you two to have something in common."

I look at her like she's crazy.

"Scratch that."

She lays her head on the open window as we fly down the road toward the lake to get us a good spot before people with suntan lotion and beach toys and their jelly-faced kids take up the whole sand trap.

It's spring break and stupid hot for late March.

But it's Ohio. Tomorrow it could be snowing, so you got to grab what you can in the time it's given to you. In a few minutes Alice has slowed down, and we're in line with about a few hundred other cars.

Marley looks at me, and I know we didn't leave early enough. We turn the radio up and inch along for about twenty more minutes until I see somebody selling barbecue on the side of the road. We pull over.

We sit on top of Alice and eat sausage po'boys as the traffic keeps crawling.

We see some people from Heaven and wave and point and laugh at them for being where we were a little while ago. After throwing down two po'boys each we hang out with the barbecue man and talk about summer. He's short and round with a soft voice. He waves toward a travel trailer parked nearby when he needs something. Then

Angela Johnson

one of his grandkids comes out and gives him more sauce, vinegar, and water or whatever.

Me and Marley talk with Chuck until the traffic speeds up. But we know the beach is packed.

Chuck waves us away with po'boys to go and a couple of bags of chips.

We head back home but have to stop the truck on the side of Route 306 to get out and dance to a song we'd been whining that we hadn't heard on the radio the whole day.

After that we're okay with everything.

I drive for the woods.

"Let's hang out on the porch and count the groundhogs," Marley says.

I laugh and nod my head. Hell, it beats jelly-faced, sticky, sunblocked kids walking all over you.

I'm pulling up into the long driveway when I see a car about thirty feet in front of me. I have to brake fast, 'cause I'm used to flying up the drive. Nobody but me ever uses it.

Two men in uniforms are knocking on the front door.

Marley says, "What's up—you join up and not tell me?"

A cool breeze breaks through the heat and freezes me to Alice's seat. I see that Curtis isn't home yet. After the two men talk to me, I'm glad he's not home. Curtis is AWOL, and it would have been a long-assed time before I saw him again. He would have been arrested at the door. A few minutes later I swear I see Curtis leaning against a tree out back. But I blink, and he's gone.

Angela Johnson

Swimming the Pacific

12

ONCE MY GIRL MARLEY COUNTED THE steps from her house to Ma's Superette. I guess we didn't have that much to do back then. Why else would she need to actually count the footsteps to a place we practically lived? She says she doesn't remember how many steps there were, but she wrote it down somewhere.

Now when I drive past Ma's, I only stop at Marley's and remember the steps I used to take when the center of town was our whole lives.

Now I watch from my truck as screaming little kids swoop down the slide on the playground in the middle of town.

Now I roll past my parents' house, always slow down just as I come to the driveway—but never stop.

I put my cigarette out in the ashtray and swear it's the last one I'll ever smoke. Until the next time, I guess. Then I pull my truck Alice over and jump out just as a school bus flies by. My stomach catches for a second, but I keep walking across the street.

I creep into the shop. Nelly's rapping on the radio, and there's too much orange air freshener smelling up the place.

"What's up, girl?"

"Nothing."

"Glad you've decided to come to work. You know those people from the state do actually show up here sometimes to check on you."

Jos has got his feet up on the cash register in his go-to-work, play, everyday jeans and a T-shirt that says STUPOR. I smile and go into the back of the store and start opening boxes. Late again, and he still hasn't fired me, 'cause he knows what that would mean. For me, school. For him, not getting cheap labor.

For true Jos is all right. He's letting me do the vocational thing here, and that's okay by me, 'cause I only have two classes a day, and that's about all I can stand.

Jos really doesn't need to worry, because ain't nobody from school's gonna push it. That

Angela Johnson

would mean me in class full time, and nobody wants that. I know the school doesn't—and I'm in agreement.

I keep unpacking boxes as Jos sets a cup of coffee beside my foot and goes back to the front of the store to answer the phone.

After a while I've unpacked a box of candles, two boxes of fairy wings—a sure sign of Halloween coming—and some throws that are the softest things I ever felt. Before I know it, I'm wrapped up in a gray one, sitting in the back room, missing the warmth of Curtis's skin, and wanting a cigarette.

And the funny thing is, I just saw him thirty minutes ago.

But things have been sliding somewhere dark since the army reserves showed up looking for him.

He never said a word, and I didn't tell him. The groundhogs got his attention for the rest of the night.

And I know something. I know the feeling, 'cause it's not too long since I had it myself. I think Curtis is already gone. Back to Iraq or wherever. He's slipping away—quietly, as usual.

13

"I USED TO WATCH THE NEWS, BUT IT WAS always changing, and I could never follow the story."

Quote from a lady on a bus I once rode to Cincinnati.

14

IF I THOUGHT IT WOULD DO ANY GOOD, I'd lay on my horn until the person who boxed me in looks out a store window and decides to come move their ride. But I know I won't be getting out anytime soon, so I climb on top of my truck, light up, and lie on the hood looking up at the clouds.

In a minute warm hands are running up my bare legs, tickling them.

The hands take my cigarette, put it out against a telephone pole by the car, then throw it in the storm sewer since there's no trash can nearby.

"Damn—can't I even have a bad habit?"

"You got more than anybody I know."

Marley's little brother, Butchy, climbs up next to me.

"What up?" he asks.

I miss my cigarette but don't light up another. I want Butchy to stay and hang for a while. At least lie on the old hoopty with me so I don't look like a stone-cold lone loser.

I smile at him.

"Yo—again, what are we doing stretched out on your ride?"

"Stupid parker," I finally say.

Butchy sits up to look at the brand-new car wedged up against Alice, then lies back beside me.

"Remember Mike Boyd's cousin Darnell?"

"Yeah, he was funny as hell that summer he stayed with Mike and we all hung out. He's crazy fun."

"You know he got shipped out."

I feel a twinge in my stomach.

Butchy looks up. "He got hurt. He was on patrol, and his carrier ran over an IED. They say he'll be home soon."

I don't know how long we lie there watching clouds blow by and listening to people calling out to each other. It seems like a whole day, 'cause we don't talk, and it's the best afternoon I've had in a long time.

The bank is closing when a man in a suit, dragging files on luggage wheels, looks over at us and gets in the car that's held me hostage for hours. Because I didn't have anywhere else to be, I wave to him, then blow a kiss.

Butchy laughs so hard he almost rolls off the truck.

When Alice is free, Butchy jumps down, ready to go. He looks down the street, then at me.

"It's pretty bad about Darnell, huh?"

I nod my head and look up the street too.

Then Butchy leaves, and the clouds cover the sun again, and there's nobody on the street anymore. I can even hear the signal light clicking the change from yellow to red.

And it's true I got nothing to do and no place to go in a hurry.

I look across the street to Ma's Superette and put my keys in my pocket. Haven't been in Ma's in a long time. . . . But just as I get to the door, I get a real warm feeling. When I look in and see the barrel of flip-flops and bin of beach toys, I turn back.

I look down at my hiking boots and start walking and counting steps from Ma's Superette to my parents' house, and I think about a boy I only knew one summer.

15

CURTIS FOUND A LETTER OUT BY THE dump one day when we went for a walk. Curtis saw the letter fluttering in the wind, leaned down, and picked it up.

I don't think I ever heard him laugh so hard. He kept the letter in his wallet. Now it's in my back pocket. I wanna remember that day and the way we both laughed.

Grace,
    I have been thinking of you for so very long. It's sad to me that things have not worked out for us. I had dreams that we would be together forever. I never thought it all would

end so quickly or hurt so deeply. I
blame myself.

I should not have let others be
more important than you. Truly I don't
think I ever realized how wonderful you
were. Yes, I was hurt when you burned
my garage down with my two cars in it.
Yes, I was surprised when I went to
the bank and you had cleaned out the
savings account.

And yes, I know people in the
neighborhood must have been talking
about how you threw all my clothes out
the front door, drove to Harry Fuel
and Eats for a can of gas, and lit
everything on fire. And most definitely,
my family will never invite you to
another get-together (me either, I guess)
after you told everybody (in detail)
the little things I say about them to
make fun.

But Grace, I forgive you
everything—if you'll just come back to
me and Buddy (who no longer tries to
bite me like you trained him to).
Love,
John

sweet, hereafter   337

By the time Jos finishes reading the letter, me and Brodie are almost crying in pain from laughing. I try to take another sip of lemonade and stretch out on the lounge chair.

We're sitting in Jos's backyard surrounded by ugly yard crap. His mom collects it. So we sit pretending we're on a beach in Hawaii, chillin' with wooly sheep and little Dutch girls. And one of those shadow men who lean against trees—just creepy.

We have the backyard to ourselves 'cause Jos says his mom hasn't actually used it since his dad left in 1982. She just likes to fill it with junk.

But we're still laughing.

"You wrote that yourself, girl," says Jos, still giggling and wiping tears.

"I didn't; I swear I didn't."

Brodie covers his head with a beach towel, then gets up.

"I'm going for a swim," he says. Then he steps in the wading pool.

"Love don't last forever," I say.

"For real," Jos grunts, and Brodie keeps pretending he's swimming in the Pacific.

Angela Johnson

16

CURTIS IS STILL ASLEEP WHEN I LEAVE FOR
school—on a Sunday. I lay my head on his
smooth back and listen to him breathing for a
minute. Then I'm out the door speeding down
country roads, 'cause I'm going to be late.

It's too hot to be inside today—but here we all
are. It's too hot to think about a future doing
this or doing that. Too hot . . .

I watch Brodie as he leans against the gym
wall and starts to read pamphlets he's picked
up from the tables. The halls are packed. And
I don't want to be here. But I've got to get my
slip signed by at least three of the people sitting
behind tables trying to convince a whole group
of sleepy kids that they want to have careers.

Marley walks over with a cup of coffee in her hand.

"How ya been?"

And that "How ya been?" is really about ten questions but she lets it slide when I answer.

"Okay."

Okay.

She puts her arm around me, and we lean on each other while we decide what fake careers we want to be interested in.

I'm thinking I want to be a fake veterinarian. Or even a fake IT person. Marley thinks she wants to be a fake college dropout and make her parents real proud. I look for Brodie, but he's gone. I wonder what fake career he's getting to snag enough signatures.

I give it up after my fake career as a vet is busted up before I even get started.

Allergies. But at least the woman signed my slip.

We walk around eating popcorn—free. Drinking pop—not free—until I see Brodie off in a corner sitting next to two men in uniforms. Their hair is crew cut and their shoes shine under the fluorescent lights. Even though it's warm, their jackets stay on, and they look crisp and cool. Too cool.

Angela Johnson

But it's not just Brodie. There's about ten boys that I know all sitting around and listening like they never listen to anything else.

I wonder how they got in.

Then I imagine I see the darkest eyes ever. Was he one of these boys not so long ago? Probably.

There are tear streaks.

First it's hot and a summer day.

And then I see the darkest eyes . . .

The darkest eyes.

I sit in front of the army recruiting office after leaving the career fair, and the sun is so hot I think I'm gonna pass out. I should just take my ass back to the woods and Curtis—but here I am. There's a glare coming off the windshield, and I have to tilt my head a certain way to get a good look at the recruiting office.

I lean across the seat and pop the glove compartment. I burn myself on the hinge, then pull out a pair of Curtis's aviator sunglasses. They slide down my nose. I turn on the radio and wait.

There are only so many locks in the world, but most of them are no match for somebody who knows an Angry Goth Boy who knows someone who has keys to get in any building downtown.

Thanks, Angry Goth Boy.

I drag the plastic garbage bag full of army brochures, pens, and blank notepaper through the alley behind the bank. Everybody uses the alleys between the stores downtown as shortcuts coming from school. I know every turn. I know the easiest ways and the nearest escapes (from skipping class with Carl).

The best Dumpster this time is at Singing Sam's Pizza.

I make sure nobody sees or hears me while I drag the bag past the back door and want pizza— but I have to finish this. Right now. I throw it in the Dumpster, change my mind about pizza, and walk back to Alice.

The sun isn't as hot when I turn on some old Tupac, push the sunglasses back up, and head back to the woods and Curtis.

17

THAT FIRST NIGHT I LIVED IN THE CABIN with Curtis, I slept all alone. After I turned Alice toward the gap in the trees, I slept in the big bed with the scary wooden gargoyles carved on the ends of the headboard, my box of jeans beside me on the floor. Curtis gave me hot chamomile tea, then took a blanket from a wooden chest at the foot of the bed and went to sleep on the couch.

I still don't know why he let me stay.

I gotta admit he was the only person I had ever even looked at. He had the darkest eyes. I loved him. I already knew it.

I loved him the day I dropped that big-assed box of T-shirts at Jos's and he was buying wings for his sister. I didn't think I'd ever see him again after he and his family moved away and left their house stone empty.

I looked.

Everybody did, 'cause they just seemed to disappear.

But that day I dropped a big-assed box on my foot, Curtis helped Jos ice my foot, and all I wanted to do was touch his beautiful brown face. And I almost did. But it felt too crazy—even for me.

His T-shirt said HIRAM COLLEGE and the only thing he said to me was, "You okay?"

After they put ice on my foot, he took his wings and left.

If you asked me now, I'd say we just ran into each other accidentally.

If asked now, I'd say that's just the way it was supposed to be.

We sat next to each other in a movie—Brodie, Marley, and Butchy on the one side of me. And three guys with Hiram colors on the other side of him.

I smiled and he asked about my foot.

Then he gave me a dollar at the carnival to win Butchy a kangaroo that I swore looked just like him. Butchy, that is. I was fishing for change, and there he was. Then he was gone.

Later he was buying birdseed at the hardware store when I came in looking for two-sided tape to put a poster up.

Our last run-in was when he pulled alongside me on the road when Alice decided to run out of gas.

He said, "If you're okay to come to my house, I live up the road. I think I have enough gas to get you and your truck home. Or stay here and I'll be back in a minute."

I'm not crazy—even though he had the darkest eyes, that didn't mean he wasn't a serial killer.

I waited.

He smiled, left, disappeared into some trees and bushes about one hundred yards up the road, and came back a few minutes later with gas. We were both happy that Alice was so old she wasn't fuel-injected and needed a gas station.

As I pulled away he said, "Good night, Sweet."

And I said, "Later, Curtis."

Curtis loved to sit in an old rocking chair and read books on the porch of the cabin. He said his uncle stayed here when he was hunting; now the place belongs to Curtis. When it got dark, he brought out candles—and at first the only thing I was thinking was he was going to mess up his eyes and would go blind. . . . (Does every thing your mama says stick?)

But soon enough when I got home from Jos's or from school, I'd be on the cabin porch with or without him—reading.

And I didn't go hungry, 'cause I ate whatever he put in front of me.

Reading and eating—that's mostly what we did in the beginning.

One night might be corn on the cob with lots of melted butter and black pepper, sliced tomatoes, and some Lake Erie fish he'd bought from some man up the road with an ice chest and fishing lures all over him.

Another night it might be sweet corn bread, red beans and rice with sweet onions, and sun tea—honey sweetened. I'd watched him from the window shirtless and barefoot take the huge canning jar out one morning, fill it, and put it in a sunny spot by the wild roses.

But the dinner I remember most was the wild salad filled with fruit and nuts and some kind of sweet creamy dressing that made me want to eat it by the bowlful. Then we crunched crusty bread that was moist and buttery inside— Curtis talked about poetry and fishing.

That night, after eighteen nights, we shared the big bed, and I fell asleep next to him.

This poem fell out of a book about the history of the buffalo soldiers.

I am too young to have gone
to seven funerals this past year.
I have stopped wearing black
because the Ohio heat
rips through me to
cook me to
the bone.

Three classmates at one time
nine months ago
when their car flipped over.
Three
separate
funerals.
A cousin's heart gave out in front
of his whole family.
Graveside
services
only.

A girl who was my
first crush
lost a brother
to the pipe.
They had to carry
her mom out the church.

And during a cold
snap one of our
neighbors slept
forever because of a faulty
heater.

And I thought that
would be the end
of it all.
Death
and said so to my
grandma.
But she looked at me with red eyes
that said
it
was
only
the beginning.

Angela Johnson

18

CURTIS LOVES TO WALK THROUGH THE woods. But I have a fever and don't think I can make this walk. Earlier, all I wanted to do was curl up on the bathroom floor and feel the cool of the toilet bowl just as I was about to throw up again. I got to know the bathroom real good.

Curtis stood outside the door and every few minutes asked how I was doing.

I didn't answer. Didn't have to.

He could hear me hurl, and I guess that was enough for him to know I was still alive.

At first he'd shadowed me. He stood behind me to make sure I didn't fall in the toilet. But after my second dive—even I got to be embarrassed that he was seeing me in the toilet bowl.

You'd think being that kind of sick would make a person lose all kind of modesty—a word I learned from my mom, but not usually in my dictionary.

Not so.

Curtis was still walking around upright 'cause he didn't go "old-food-in-the-refrigerator diving" with me. I didn't eat anything green or blue, but I guess I was off by a week or so about how old some of it was.

Even though I still feel sick as a dog, I go into the woods with Curtis anyway.

His arms are wrapped around my shoulders while I suck water out of a bottle and hope he'll walk slow. He does—and keeps asking if I should be resting. He could show me what he wanted to later, when I feel better (which is to say when I'm too empty to throw up anymore). I now take the walk as a dare and say so.

He laughs.

We walk over fallen trees and go off the path by the creek. Most of the underbrush is mossy from lack of sunshine.

I'm starting to feel a bit better.

Don't want to throw up at all now.

We keep walking, though—and I squeeze his hand hard and look up through the leaves on

Angela Johnson

the trees. I can see the sun trying to shine down through them. The trees look damned tall as I gaze up, but we go farther in the woods, and it gets darker and cooler, until finally I can't hear the creek or any crickets.

The woods are as quiet as the first minutes of sleep.

But I am with Curtis, his hand around mine, when the old wooden shack appears between two old oaks. I look at Curtis, but I never ask why we're here. It ain't like me.

Scares me when I think about how much I sometimes think not like me anymore.

But I trust him, and being sick doesn't help. Maybe I'm just too damned tired to question as we stand outside the old wooden shack with the flat roof. Wildflowers grow around it—tiny flowers that appear purple in the twilight. Curtis opens the door and pulls me into the dirt-floor shack—I look around and step back out. Curtis follows me.

"It's an old storage shack. My pops's friends used to keep their extra rifles locked up in here when they were out in the woods."

"I like it. It reminds me of the cabin, only miniature."

The moon streams down through a clearing in the trees and comes down right beside the little shack. Curtis pulls a blanket out of his pack and puts it down against a wall so I can lean against it. Then he sits down beside me. I lean against him, and he feels my forehead.

"Ooh—fever germs," he says.

I rub my face against his. "A few sick cooties for you . . ."

Curtis closes his eyes.

"I dreamed about this, ya know."

"You dreamed about me having a fever and you dragging me into the woods to an old storage shack?"

"No, no. I dreamed about coming back here when I was over there."

"Oh," I say.

"I dreamed of rain, pine trees, and these woods. Sometimes I almost started to think that real color didn't exist anymore. I mean, you don't see wildflowers like these in the desert."

He runs his hands over the carpet of purple flowers surrounding us and the shack. Curtis barely ever wants to talk about Iraq, so I listen quietly.

"I dreamed about sitting on the porch. I dreamed about the quiet. I don't think I've ever missed this quiet so much. The quiet of birds chirping and midnight train whistles. There was another kind of quiet in Iraq. A quiet I never got used to.

"And sometimes you could almost feel when something was gonna happen. I mean, you knew. You felt it coming."

I want to ask him if he was scared most of the time—but I stop myself, because I figure it's a stupid question. Who wouldn't be scared with people trying to kill them?

So I just say— "You need to stay home and sit on your porch."

Curtis gets up and starts pacing in front of me; then I guess he remembers where he is and sits down to soak in the woods and the quiet.

"I don't want to go back, but if I have to—I have to. It's me or some other poor fool."

"Why can't it be nobody?" I say.

Curtis feels my head.

"Are you delusional?"

"No—just hopeful and pissed, I guess."

Curtis laughs, but I've seen him happier, or maybe I really am delusional.

He lies back on the blanket, and I sprinkle grass on him.

"I dreamed about this. I really dreamed about just being here, and it was perfect, just like it is now. I don't want anything else. No food, no house. I just want to be here. It's perfect, Sweet. I could die here just like this."

19

WHEN CURTIS STARTED SCREAMING IN HIS sleep, it was like the end of the world.

At first he would just breathe hard in his sleep. Usually it would stop there. Or he'd wake himself up. But mostly it was just the breathing hard.

I'd watch him until his breath slowed.

It was no big deal at first. Just a dream. Maybe a nightmare.

But then the screaming started, and on top of that it looked like he was trying to carry something in his hand. All I could do was try to wake him up. It was hard to do that. Especially with him screaming for people to stop or run or help him take something away.

When he finally did wake up, he'd complain that his arms hurt.

He'd say— "Man—my arms are sore."

Then he'd look over at me next to him like he was asking me if I knew the reason. And I could have told him that it looked to me that in his dream he was always trying to pick something up.

I could have told him that, but I didn't.

I didn't, because I wouldn't have been able to stop there. I would have wanted to know when the dreams started and were they because of something that happened over there in Iraq (which he never wanted to talk about). So when he finally tries to get to sleep again, this time I just lie beside him and stare into the dark until I only hear his slow breathing and the creek outside.

I should ask him about the nightmares.

But I don't think that will keep them away. And when it comes to bad dreams, all anybody ever wants is for them to stay away.

A letter from my mama:

> Sweet,
>
> I wanted to send you this on your birthday, but it didn't seem like something you would appreciate. I haven't really

found that thing, have I? But I promise, I think about you all the time. You are never out of my mind.

I know that you are still going to school and working at your friend's store. I know because I check up on you. I have not left you completely.

But I knew I had to let you go. You've been leaving since you were born. I could never put my arms around you enough to get you to stay. I guess I could have continued forcing you like I have been doing all these years. But I can't do that anymore. You have made up your mind.

I trust that you are happier where you are than you were with us.

Are you?

Are you understood? Do you laugh more? Does this young man

Angela Johnson

make you know that you are loved?

Everyone, your father included, thinks I'm crazy for not dragging you back. But they don't understand. You'd run further and faster. At least this way you are within my heart's reach. And my hands if they might be helpful or needed.

Do you drive by the house? I think I see you sometimes.

Do you? I hope so.

Maybe one day you will drop by, come in, or just come back. . . .

Love,

Mama

Come and Gone

20

I GAVE BUTCHY A RIDE HOME FROM school and talked to Marley for a few minutes, then—'cause Marley said he'd asked about me—drove over to Bobby's to check out him and Feather. It was a good day.

I even stopped and talked to my brother Jason, who was coming out of the drugstore. I pulled over and opened Alice's door for him to get in and talk a bit. And to save my life I don't know what we talked about.

But it made me happy as I drove on back to the woods and Curtis. And when I got back to Curtis and the cabin, the place smelled good. Food was cooking, and Curtis was smiling and singing as I put my car keys on top of an official-looking opened envelope.

I got a twinge 'cause I was so happy right then. I got a twinge 'cause I was feeling a little guilty. I never told Curtis about the soldiers who showed up. Maybe he knows, though. Maybe he saw them coming. Maybe he watched them and me from the woods. He's not a fool. He knows he's AWOL. But I don't want to break everything up now.

I just can't.

Curtis had put on some zydeco music I'd never heard but liked a lot.

He kept looking at me. Dark-eyed. Dark-eyed and smiling.

Every now and then he'd remember the groundhog bowl and put vegetable peels in it.

"So what do you want for dinner?" he asked.

"Whatever you got in the oven or on the stove," I laughed. He always asked. I'd eat the wood off the side of the cabin if somebody put cheese on it. I love to eat.

We ate, talked, and laughed. And after that I helped him clear the table and wash the dishes. When we were done, we sat on the couch entwined and listened to the woods.

There were long arms all around me, and I just knew I was going to get in trouble for not getting home. Then I remembered this was home and fell back to sleep. When I woke up again, he wasn't there.

I looked everywhere in the cabin, then out in the yard.

I was barefoot and felt the chill.

But I decided to keep looking for him.

It's pitch dark in the woods when I finally come out. My feet are so cold it's like they aren't even attached to me as I watch them scratched and bleeding. And if I looked in a mirror, I know my hair would be full of leaves and who knows what.

I walk through the front door and drop the flashlight on the couch.

I remember the groundhogs and take their scraps out to them. I feel like I'm sleepwalking, though.

The couch is calling me, 'cause I know I can't sleep in the bed. I ache.

I decide I'll ache on the couch or maybe not in the cabin at all. When I walk over to the table to get my keys, I knock all the mail off, and a letter floats to my feet from the army.

I read it, drop it, then curl up on the couch and listen to the leaves blowing in the breeze outside and think about how I feel that I might never be warm again but don't have the strength to go get a blanket.

When I wake the sun is dragging itself from behind some clouds, and there's a blanket around me, but in my heart I know I am all alone, even if I can't remember if I covered myself in the first place.

Angela Johnson

21

BRODIE ISN'T IN CLASS TODAY. EVERYBODY is saying it has something to do with cops and career day. And I think about my criminal activity on career day and wonder what Brodie might have done.

I don't even want to start guessing. Everybody in this school is so bored they make up half the stuff they say. But I do start to wonder where Brodie is. I miss him at lunch when no one comes up and eats half the bad food that's on my tray.

I miss him in Jameson's class, 'cause I don't have anybody to pass notes to or egg on to disrupt the class before I pass out from boredom. Angry Goth Boy has been a real disappointment lately.

Maybe he's on medication. He wears a lot less black.

Lately.

Too bad.

It's sad to see a body stop raging into the dying of any light.

Sorry, Angry Goth Boy.

The halls have emptied out for fourth period, and I'm late as usual when I see Brodie walking slow down the other end of the hall. I wave to him, then slide down against my locker to wait for him. In about a minute he's sitting next to me on the floor.

"I'm heading to the store," I say.

Brodie takes off his sunglasses.

"Good I saw you before you broke out. . . ."

He takes a banana out of his shoulder bag, starts to peel it, then offers me a bite.

I say, "Nope—too banana."

He snorts.

I snort back.

"So what's up with everybody talking about something happening to you with career day?"

"Damn! These people must have spies on every corner." Brodie jumps up and looks under his arms. "Do I got bugs on me or what?"

I smile, and he sits back down beside me.

"What do you have to kill around here to get a little privacy?"

"Boredom," I say.

Brodie nods and finishes his banana.

"So why you creepin' in?"

He puts the peel back into his bag and fishes out an apple and a bottle of orange juice. He takes a swig of juice and starts laughing.

"The cops, the army, and my old man."

"Oh, shit, Brodie—you didn't join, did you?"

Brodie doesn't say a word. He just sits there eating his apple and drinking. When he's done, he takes his sunglasses out of his bag, puts them on, and stares at me.

"Ya know, Sweet girl, it's like you don't know me at all. . . ."

Then he gets up and smiles down at me and says—

"You should find a better Dumpster than the pizza parlors. I'd find something more toward the township."

I look up at him.

Then Brodie walks toward class, turns around, shrugging, and yells—

"I'm just saying . . ."

And it's like I don't know him all over again—but like him more than almost anybody.

When I finally get to bed tonight, I listen to the creek and imagine the groundhogs underneath the cabin. I listen for Curtis, who hasn't been back since the night I read the letter from the army. . . .

Now when I come home from work and school I go for walks along the edge of the woods, cook because I want to get used to it, or get in Alice and drive around town.

Sometimes I go by Jos's house and listen to him and his mother annoy each other after he's closed the store.

Yesterday I hung out with his mother, Willa, who makes me laugh and is a whole lot more crazy than anyone I've ever met.

She yells for me to come in when I knock and ask if Jos is home.

"Come on in, honey. Jos went to Cleveland to pick up something from a supplier. Some woman who makes charms or something—I don't know."

I walk into the living room, and she's knitting.

There's yarn—everywhere.

Jos's mom has a graying curly Afro, weighs about eighty pounds, and is what my mom would call a serious hippie chick. But I wouldn't say that. I think she's living in the here and now even though Jos was born in a commune.

"Sit, kid," she says, and pushes about twenty balls of yarn out of the butterfly chair.

So I just sit and watch her knit.

"Tea," she says after a while, and I say, "I'll get it"—and do.

Willa puts down her knitting and starts drinking her tea.

"Good tea, kid."

"Thanks."

Then she stares at me for a long time. Jos told me way before I met her that she was always trying to see inside people's souls. Freaky.

"You happy?"

Okay—that shit shocks me, 'cause I was just thinking how I wasn't. . . . I don't want to lie, so I say, "Sometimes."

She picks up her knitting again. "Well, sometimes—sometimes has to be enough."

"I always thought so," I say.

"Maybe you ought to go back home. Maybe you miss your family."

I say, "Maybe." And then think about my

brothers at home. "But I don't think so—I'm all right where I am."

Willa nods her head and turns to look out the window.

"Well, from everything I've heard, you'll be okay with that Wright boy. Knew his family before they left for parts unknown. Nice. And he seems lovely and sincere."

I take a roll of yarn in my hand and start squeezing it.

"Have you ever met him?"

Willa laughs. "As a matter of fact he drove me and a couple of my friends to a demonstration out by the campus. Parking was gonna be a mess, and we didn't want to get towed. He overheard a few of my girlfriends and me in the coffee shop talking. He offered to take us, 'cause he had a parking permit. He actually drove us there in his uniform and was waiting for us by his car when it was all over.

"Amazing young man. Lovely, sad, but amazing."

I squeeze the soft pink yarn harder.

"Yes, yes he —is. . . ."

She stares at me again while I start to wrap the yarn around my fingers.

In and around.

Angela Johnson

After a while Willa starts talking about her volunteer work and how impossible it is to get anything organic in Heaven after the summer vegetable stands close up. And she's really sick of having to haul ass to another cute overpriced market in one of the rich suburbs.

I feel warm and safe when she talks, and I pour myself more tea and get lost in her world of feeding the homeless, antiwar protests, and the never-ending quest for food that won't eventually kill you. I like Willa. And when she talks about anything and everything, it smoothes over the fact that I will have to go back to a place that I love—but that is quiet and lonely.

Lonely and quiet.

And it's going to be that way until it isn't anymore.

The evening sun starts to go down while I listen to the calm and Willa.

22

SO THE STORY IS (AND EVERYBODY THINKS they know it by now) that I either ran away or was kicked out of my parents' house for drugs, drinking, being pregnant, or—if you listen to the most messed-up story—all of them. After all these months of living in the cabin people just now are asking what happened! And when it looks like somebody is going to ask me, I just stare right through 'em and dare them to ask.

Nobody has so far.

So the bullshit just keeps rolling down the hill, and I don't do anything to stop it.

Why?

Why not?

Curtis says people like to be knee-deep in it anyway.

I say it makes 'em feel better about their boring lives when they think of a tragic one for somebody else. We love to hear the tragic stories. The news is full of them, and it makes me feel good that I live where I never have to watch it.

And when I'm just walking around the cabin in one of Curtis's old shirts, going window to window—I miss that he was here. His smell. His touch.

Him.

Maybe Willa is right about me going home, but then I walk to a shelf and pull out a book and get lost in it and I don't have to think about anything else.

The story is about a girl alone in the woods who left home 'cause she couldn't be happy there no matter how she or anybody else tried to make it so.

I go window to window, and the story never changes.

To the Bone

23

CURTIS HAS NOT COME HOME. THE woods did not give him up the night I almost froze looking for him. But who do I tell? What do I do? In a breath you can be gone from this place—anyplace. And the only thing you leave behind is what you meant to someone.

Curtis hardly ever talks—but the night that he left, he talked more than I'd ever heard him before. Was it a gift?

The first few days I went to school and tried not to think about it. I believed he'd be back. Quiet and sad, maybe, but he'd be back. He is not back, and maybe after a while I'll have to do something else to look for him.

• • •

For a long time—there were no caskets. Not one. Not one to be photographed, not one to 'cause pain, not one to make people remember.

Where were the caskets?

I want all the yellow ribbons to disappear off of big-assed SUVs.

I want people to stop waving flags like it makes them better than people who don't.

I want never to hear one more word about being patriotic—'cause most of them don't even know what the hell patriotism is.

I want to sit in class and not think that some of the people around me might end up shooting or getting shot at by people they'd never know.

The new president now says we can see the caskets come home.

Good.

What if everybody starts forgetting that people are dying again, even with the caskets?

What if everybody fuckin' forgets?

Because there are caskets now, and people still forget.

And what if everybody just starts paying attention to something else and never cares 'cause they've never taken the time to see the caskets?

Angela Johnson

24

BRODIE AND JOS TAKE TO THE COURT
after seven little elementary kids in a pickup
game finish fighting over their basketball for
about the hundredth time. All three of us
were leaning against the fence and laughing
until about a minute ago, when Brodie took
the basketball and shot it up into the tree
overhanging the court.

Damn—little kids shouldn't cuss—but Jos
and Brodie just laugh harder at them while they
wait for their ball to fall. It doesn't, and they
finally give up waiting. A couple of them are
still talking smack as they walk away down the
sidewalk.

I take a couple of free shots and make all of
them, but then lose interest and let Brodie and

Jos have the ball they brought to the court with them.

A few minutes after they start playing, the other basketball finally falls out of the tree and rolls toward me on the other side of the court. I think about chasing the kids to give it back but change my mind, get up, and hide it behind the weeds by the tree.

Maybe they'll think about looking over there if they come back.

It's hard to lose things.

"So what's it about, anyway? Except for the obvious," Brodie says after making about twenty one-handed layups and jogging around the court.

I know he's talking to me, 'cause Jos stopped playing about a half hour ago and is reading a graphic novel now with his iPod probably turned high enough to make him deaf for a couple of days.

Brodie sits down on the court beside me.

I smile. "Do we ever talk to each other in chairs anymore?"

Brodie throws the basketball up in the air and lets it roll off the court. "True dat . . ."

"So what do you wanna know?"

Brodie stretches his legs out.

"Crimes, girl. Crimes against military brochures, locks, military premises."

"It wasn't that much. But how come you know so much? You moved too fast the other day to tell me anything."

"Somebody saw me in the neighborhood around the time you committed your little civil disobedience."

"Why were you there?"

"Hangin' out."

"Downtown—on a Sunday. Everything is closed."

"Uh-huh."

I look at Brodie and finally get it.

"You were following me?"

"Damn, Sweet, sometimes you are seriously slow. I worry about you—a lot lately. You're in some kind of daze. Where you at?"

"Fine—I'm okay Brodie."

"Just fine—or okay?" he says.

"You are getting on my nerves now."

Brodie just nods at me, then walks over to the basketball and shoots it one-handed. I remember the summer he wore his right hand in a sling so he could learn how to shoot left-handed. He's good any way he shoots now.

Jos is still reading and ignoring us.

Brodie pops a few from the corner a few times, then moves back far enough for three points and makes it. Then he goes to the free-throw line and shoots until he misses.

The sun's starting to go down, and in a minute the street-lights will start coming on. I hear somebody's mother calling them down the street, a dog barking, and a car starting up across the road from the courts. It's all the sounds I didn't think I would ever miss after moving out to the woods. But I do—sometimes now.

Just sometimes.

Jos closes his book, takes out his earphones in time enough for Brodie to ask, "Where is he, Sweet? Where's your boy Curtis?"

Angela Johnson

25

I CLEANED THE CABIN FROM TOP TO bottom the day after Curtis left. I mean, I didn't just clean it; I scrubbed it. Hard. With an old scrub brush I found under the kitchen sink that looked about a hundred years old.

I used soap, bleach, pine cleaner. Anything I could find.

I called Jos and told him I was sick. I never miss work. I could mess it all up, missing anything about school—even though me and Jos are cool. Sometimes the school checks your vocational employers. They just show up.

I scrubbed the floors.

The walls.

The bathroom.

I scrubbed the front porch, too.

Everything in me told me he wasn't coming back. I just knew it. I knew it 'cause he was disappearing every day that I was there and had probably started way before I ever left home. And anyway, he'd never promised me anything—just a home for a while. That's it.

We hadn't known each other long enough to love each other.

And I hadn't known him well enough, period.

So I scrubbed until my hands felt raw to the bone.

And even though I'd dream about his arms and eyes and sometimes forget he was gone and imagine that I heard him—I knew.

I knew he was gone forever.

Brodie and Jos read the letter from the army, and there's this part of me says that the letter is private, meant only for Curtis. Or his family. But they aren't here. They're all in Texas now.

"So they were sending him back." Jos is shaking his head.

I walk over to the couch, sit, and look out the window.

Brodie says, "I guess in a while they'll

be sending out the MPs to get him for going AWOL—huh?"

"He's not AWOL," I say.

Brodie and Jos look at me, then at the letter again.

It's the first time I've let anybody in the cabin since Curtis left. I thought anybody would be able to tell like I did that he was gone. It no longer smells or feels like he ever lived here. I mean—there are his books and music, but those could belong to anybody.

"Where do you think he went, Sweet?" Jos asks, then walks across the room and sits next to me on the couch.

I point toward the woods.

"Have you looked?" He asks.

I don't say I don't have the nerves to go back into the woods.

Brodie stands with his arms folded, staring out the window.

"It's been pretty cool at night lately."

Jos must know what he's talking about, 'cause he stands up and walks over to Brodie.

"We'll be back, okay."

"Just stay here and try to get some rest."

"Don't worry—we got this."

And in a minute they're both gone.

I watch the door closing and am left sitting on the couch looking out the window at a quiet, sunny day while Brodie and Jos go into the woods.

I walk over and take a CD from the shelf, put it in the stereo, and listen to zydeco for a little while.

Angela Johnson

Hereafter

26

I LOOK AT THE FRONT PAGE OF THE newspaper now and see Jos standing by the cop looking like an old man. They didn't take a picture of Brodie (or they did and just didn't use it).

Nobody knows it, but I was hiding in the bushes, 'cause in the end I'd listened to enough music and decided to go into the woods to look for them. They weren't in Curtis's grandpa's woods. So I kept walking.

The sun was high and hot when I finally found them, cops and EMS on the edge of the woods and blocking Route 306, about a mile past the cabin. They were loading a body into an ambulance. Jos shook his head, and the cop reached over and touched his arm.

That's when the photographer aimed her camera.

And I walked back through the woods.

Angela Johnson

27

CURTIS'S FAMILY WILL FLY HIS BODY BACK to Texas. One of his older brothers, Jules, came from Texas to take him back to his family.

I got to see Curtis at the morgue because I begged. I wasn't family, and he'd already been identified. But I begged as my mother stood beside me—this time. She held my hand as we walked into the room.

The day before Jules leaves with Curtis, he comes to the cabin. I am waiting for him. I have been waiting since the day Curtis found out he had to go back to Iraq, then knew he couldn't. I've been waiting for his family.

I'm sitting on the porch. My duffel bag is packed inside when he pulls up in what must be a rental. He's wearing a black suit and dark glasses. He takes the glasses off when he walks up the steps.

His eyes look just like Curtis's.

"Sweet?"

"Yes."

"I remember you from the old neighborhood."

I smile 'cause I can't cry anymore.

"Jules," he says, while putting his hand out for me to shake.

I do and look in his eyes.

He walks into the cabin and starts walking from room to room. Slowly and like a stranger who's never been there.

"He loved this place. He was the only one in the family who did."

Jules breathes out and starts looking at Curtis's books and music—then shakes his head.

"Did you take what you wanted?" he asks me.

"I don't need anything," I say, then hold out the key.

He looks at the key, hands me a piece of paper, then turns away and heads out the door.

"Keep it. And if you don't mind, we'll need someone to check on the cabin every now and then—if you can and don't mind."

I put the key in my back jean pocket and nod my head and read his address and phone number in Texas. In a minute he's disappeared down the driveway and out onto the road. I walk through the cabin again, only not like Jules. I know this place.

I remember the man who lived here and took me into this safe place—for a while. Then left me here when he couldn't feel safe anymore.

I sit on the front porch until the sun starts to go down. I take my bags, toss them in the back of Alice, start her up, then slowly drive through the trees.

I look back just as the first groundhog of the night comes out.

The poem Jules put in Curtis's coffin for me:

> In the sweet hereafter
> everything
> that you ever wanted
> in your heart
> will float to your
> feet.

In the sweet hereafter
everyone that you know
will know who you
are.
And your heart
will be an open book.

In the sweet hereafter
there will be no
bombs,
grenades,
IEDS,
needlessly dead
or perpetually dying boys, girls,
men, women, and babies.

In the sweet hereafter there will be
no reason—no reason at all.

Angela Johnson